THE PHILISTINES

One by one, the younger members of the Moorhouse family have decided to leave their Ayrshire farm for Victorian Glasgow. The family business in the Candleriggs is a little slow, but the clan continues to be prosperous. Phoebe is engaged, Sophia, Mary and Bel's children are growing up and Arthur is involved in charity work, but they are all drawn together when the dashing and impulsive David falls in love with Lucy Rennie, a professional singer, whose career places her far beneath his family in the social order. Far worse – David is already engaged to the charms and riches of another.

THE PHILISTINES

THE PHILISTINES

by

Guy McCrone

Magna Large Print Books
Long Preston, North Yorkshire,
BD23 4ND, England.

British Library Cataloguing in Publication Data.

McCrone, Guy
    The philistines.

    A catalogue record of this book is
    available from the British Library

    ISBN   978-0-7505-3093-4

First published in Great Britain in 1947

Copyright © 1993 Guy McCrone

Cover illustration © Len Thurston by arrangement with
P.W.A. International

The right of Guy McCrone to be identified as the author of this
work has been asserted by him in accordance with the
Copyright, Designs and Patents Act, 1988

Published in Large Print 2009 by arrangement with
Black & White Publishing Ltd.

Magna Large Print is an imprint of Library Magna Books Ltd.

Printed and bound in Great Britain by
T.J. (International) Ltd., Cornwall, PL28 8RW

Chapter One

For a few moments David Moorhouse did not realise that the play was over. The tension still held him. It was only when the curtain had swept down into its place, its golden fringe bouncing a little in the glow of the footlights, that he began once more to be conscious of his surroundings. Suddenly the storm of applause broke. Men and women were standing up in their places clapping their hands. There were whistles and shouts from the pit and the gallery. For a time the roar continued. At last the curtain trembled. The storm changed to a tempest.

Irving, lean and exhausted, was standing before them, modestly bowing his thanks.

David had never seen him before. A classical actor in a classical play wasn't much in his line, really. But he had been told that, to be in the swim, he must see Irving's Hamlet. It would be a solemn, stately affair, he had expected. He would buy a ticket for himself and go to have a look at it. After that he would be able to tell his friends he had been, and duly and suitably agree how wonderful Mr. Irving was. And now he was standing up in his seat like the others, clapping his hands off in thanks to the strange, pale creature down there in front of the footlit curtain. His equipment for judging Irving's art were his own placid emotions, a certain natural refinement, and a shallow, provincial sophistication. But that had been enough for Irving to work on.

David had gone to take part in a social ritual. Instead, he had been forced to share, and share acutely, the feelings of another young man, troubled and wearied, groping his way through indecision and corruption to a merciful death. It had all been intensely human – the last thing that he had expected. He had heard that Mr. Irving could be terrifying; that he could freeze a theatre with horror; that he could be cold, aloof and regal. But this heart-breaking, noble intimacy, this pitiless exposure of the raw places of a wounded mind, was something beyond David's experience.

As he stood in the hot theatre looking down, he found himself wondering what possible kind of person this Mr. Irving could be. What were actors like? How did they live? He had never had the slenderest contact with the world Irving belonged to. Actors and artists were strange, erratic people. That was a commonplace. And, in Glasgow at least, solid, well-doing people didn't want to know them. But now in his enthusiasm David could not help asking himself what

Mr. Irving had done to prepare himself for this performance. Had he learnt the words and trusted to his exceptional emotions? Or did he discipline himself in some way?

Irving was standing now hand in hand with his Ophelia, Miss Brennon, acknowledging the endless applause. What kind of life did that girl lead? She looked frail and gentle and not any older than David's own sister Phœbe. He had been solemnly told that actresses were exposed to all sorts of moral dangers. He could well believe it of the girls who sang in the Scotia or at Brown's. Nobody expected a girl in a free-and-easy to be a paragon. But this girl who had so well set forth for him the anguish and gentle madness of Ophelia?

David Moorhouse was hopelessly Philistine, but he belonged to a tribe whose emotions were by no means overworked and blunt. He had been much moved by a great actor in a great play, but it would have been quite beyond his powers to tell why.

II

It was late when he found himself standing at last outside the new Theatre Royal in Hope Street. There had been flurries of snow during the day. But now, though it was cold, it was dry. A long chain of cabs waited to take the wealthier of the audience home. One by one, as the doorman called out their numbers, the muffled cabmen pulled the rugs from the backs of their horses and moved to the brightly lit entrance.

Under the blazing gaselier, David had recognised more than one friend who might have offered him a lift. But he had avoided everybody. The play had thrown him into a strange, unaccountable excitement. He wanted to be left alone. For a moment he looked about him, wondering if he should go down into Sauchiehall Street and pick up a cab for himself. But almost at once he decided to walk. The theatre had been hot. The fresh air would do him good. He wanted to think. He turned into Cowcaddens and made his way towards New City Road.

He was now passing through one of the slums of the city. It was only Tuesday night, and he would have only himself to look to. Towards the end of the week, when wages came in, drinking and riot made this district impossible at so late an hour. Even tonight, as he hurried along, he passed one or two wretches staggering and roaring. Many dirty, barefoot children were still about. There was filth and squalor everywhere; and not a little misery. For in November of 1878 Glasgow was deep in trade depression. In this she was like the rest of the Kingdom. Businesses were failing everywhere. Banks were collapsing. The City Bank of Glasgow had been the first and greatest British Bank to go. Its shareholders and depositors had been the victims of fraud as well as bad times. Unemployment was mounting. There were rumours of war. Depression bred depression. And meanwhile the people suffered; just such hungry, haggard people as David was passing now.

But as he hurried along, his hands deep in his pockets and his coat-collar upturned, his thoughts were far from the people around him. One became used to the sights of everyday. The play had set his brain racing, sharpening consciousness, stimulating thought. As he paced along, he found himself living again the hours he had passed in the theatre. The wonderful traffic of the stage, with that extraordinary man at its centre. The packed auditorium; a great tribute to Mr. Irving in these bad times. The people sitting near him – well-dressed, comfortable people, taking life easily. And then, inevitably, life in general, and his own in particular. What did it all come to?

Where did he, David Moorhouse, stand? Where was he getting to?

He was pounding along New City Road now. For a long distance in front of him, beyond St. George's Cross, he could see the chain of street lamps stretching, as it seemed, to infinity. A sharp wind was blow-ing in his face. He bent his weight against it and pushed on.

He was thirty-one, unmarried, prosperous. Indeed, the whole Moorhouse clan was prosperous. The family business in the Candleriggs might be slow this autumn, but it was steady. These farmer's sons, Arthur and David Moorhouse, dealt in the produce of the farmlands; and people must eat, even in bad times. It was possible to wait for better times before commissioning a house or an Atlantic liner, but it was less easy to wait for a pound of cheese.

The foundations of his life, then, were sound, thanks to an older brother who had built the business and taken him into it. Time was when he had resented Arthur's guiding hand, but for years now he had been quite settled and able to spread his wings. The family in its increasing prosperity, had moved out West. The Moorhouses were beginning to have standing. And his, David's, social success had been greatest of all. He was reasonably handsome. He was young and he was eligible. People invited him.

He stopped for a moment at St. George's Cross, to allow traffic coming up from St. George's Road to pass him. The breath of the horses showed as puffs of white vapour in the cold air.

Yet what did it all amount to? He was just an ordinary, well-disposed young man with a facile, pleasant way with him. Nobody at all, really. But why should that matter?

David stared, taking stock. Tonight he had looked into the face of great achievement, and although it was of a kind for which he held no yardstick, it had left him dissatisfied and self-critical.

The theatre. Irving. The applause. His tangled train of thought brought him to the love of Hamlet for Ophelia, and from there it went to the question of love as it affected himself. Was love the solution of his problem; the answer to his restlessness? Would it close this void, this emptiness? Many women had asked him why he didn't marry. He had told them quite truthfully that he didn't know.

Marriage presented itself to him as a house in a terrace, a starched parlourmaid, calling-cards and a carriage. But the strange being who would have to share the carriage with him? What about her? On this strange night of quickened sensibility, David looked into himself sharply, and had to admit that he did not want to share a house, or a carriage – or a bed, for that matter – with anyone. At any rate, not permanently. And, now that he came to think of it, he never had done.

This last aspect of it troubled him. He had never been in love. No nineteen-year-old passion, even, had crushed his hopes of happiness forever. Was he abnormal? He had reason to know that he was not. Abnormal emotionally, perhaps? Too self-analytical, too apt to stand aside and note his own feelings?

III

He was coming to Kelvinbridge now. On his right hand was Rosebery Terrace, where his sister Sophia Butter and her family lived. There was still a light in a downstairs window. Should he go in and say 'Hello', just before he went back to his own bachelor quarters? Sophia at least was the family. One of his own. But he decided against it and pushed on. Sophia was a good-hearted chatterbox. But she was the last sort of person to soothe him in the mood in which he found himself tonight.

On the bridge he could hear the waters of the Kelvin rushing over the weir in the darkness below him. On the other side a third horse was being joined to a late tram-car to help to pull it up into Hillhead. In five minutes David would be home.

Did it come to this, then, that he had better get himself married, whether he was in love or not? Would it turn him into some-one? Develop him? In a year or two he would be one of the old young-men-about-town. Not a fraternity he wanted to belong to. If only he could fall in love, everything would be easy. Or so the more sentimental

14

of his married friends told him. He had never quite trusted the people who had hastened to offer him this information. People who could talk about these things tended to be shallow. Still – perhaps.

Near the top of the hill he took a street on the left, and in a few minutes more he had reached his lodgings. He let himself in with his key and turned up the gas. There was still a glow among the ashes of his fireplace. He bent down, raked the bits together and coaxed a flame from them. As he straightened himself and took off his overcoat, he examined his reflection in the great gilt mirror that filled the wall above his draped and tasselled mantelpiece. His face had more colour than usual. Wind and exercise had put it there. He pushed back his thick, chestnut hair and stroked his discreet, boyish whiskers. It was not the first time David had looked into a glass, and it was not the first time he had been pleased with the reflection. But now, tonight, it was the first time that he had caught himself wondering what kind of effect that reflection might have on the young woman, whose face as yet he could not see.

Suddenly his lips broke into a smile and he turned away. No, he didn't look so bad. Men with worse faces than that had got themselves married. So far as faces went, his chances were quite good.

But now a thought had struck him. He would go and ask Bel Moorhouse about all this. Bel would help him. Bel was pleasantly, comfortably worldly, and quite prepared for any amount of pros and cons. He would look in at Grosvenor Terrace, sometime during the coming weekend.

David pulled off his boots and thrust his feet into his embroidered slippers. Getting up, he went to his sideboard, poured himself out a tumbler of whisky and water, and settled himself by the fire. Yes, Bel was the one to discuss this. If he could make her realise that he was in earnest, perhaps she could help him.

Chapter Two

This Saturday evening Bel Moorhouse was enjoying the luxury of absenting herself from where she had decided it was proper for her to be. She had taken tickets for Herr Julius Tausch's orchestral concert in the New Public Halls in Berkeley Street. The Arthur Moorhouses were not very musical. But it was time, Bel felt, that, living as they now did in one of the smartest terraces in the West End of Glasgow, they should be seen among people of consequence and taste.

But she had been busy. Already this week they had been to see Mr. Irving in 'Louis XI', to a church social, and to spend a dull and dutiful evening with Mary McNairn. This afternoon, as she stood at one of the long windows of her pleasant first-floor drawing-room, looking out across the Botanic Gardens, cheerless and dank, she decided that home was the only place this evening. Her spirit for once had failed her. No. Her mending-basket and a seat by the fire.

She turned to find her sister-in-law standing beside her. 'Hullo, Phœbe dear.'

The sight of the young girl gave Bel pleasure, as she stood there, glowing in brown velvet and fur.

'Where have you been?'

'In Hillhead, shopping.'

A beautiful creature really, this slender child, with her slanting Highland eyes and her jet-black hair. And she had promised to marry a strange young man who had lost all his money. Pity, in a way, although Bel liked Henry Hayburn well enough.

Bel became all friendliness and briskness. 'Phœbe dear, I feel that you and Henry ought to go to the concert tonight.'

'We're too hard up.'

'But I was going to offer you our tickets. There's a new singer tonight.'

'Who?'

'An Italian name. I don't remember.' Bel

looked at the window as a blast of sleet struck the glass. 'Anyway, it's bound to be very interesting,' she added.

'I would quite like to go. At least it's something to do.'

'Very well, that's settled. You and Henry are just at a time in your lives when you should be enjoying everything you can. Arthur and I have had our fling.'

Phœbe had thanked Bel, wondering what kind of fling her hard-working brother had ever had. And so, having duly fed and packed Phœbe and her affianced husband off to the New Public Halls, Bel settled down by the fire with her sewing. There was only one thing lacking for her immediate contentment, and that was the presence of her husband. Arthur, an elder of the Ramshorn Church, was downstairs in the parlour (which Bel was trying to induce the younger members of the family to call the library) having an interminable interview with a dissatisfied church member.

It was right, of course, that anyone so upright and dependable as Arthur should be a church elder. But really, there were limits. Arthur was forever receiving calls from stuffy church people in whom she couldn't possibly be interested. And it was wonderful what they could go on being dissatisfied about. If only Arthur would stop being so conscientious. Bel rooted crossly in the

18

mending-basket. She had arranged a quiet Saturday evening for him. Now it was being spoilt by dissatisfaction.

The solution was, of course, for Arthur and his family to leave the Ramshorn and join a church in this new and fashionable suburb of Kelvinside. It was tiresome to make the long journey into the City every Sunday. Especially when you might be going to a smart church not ten minutes away; a church with a bright, modern minister, who would keep your ideas abreast of the times, and bright, modern members who bought their wives entertaining hats, and had other, more up-to-date hobbies than dissatisfaction.

There was the sound of someone moving in the hall downstairs. It must be Arthur's visitor going. That was better.

She did not even turn her head as the drawing-room door opened, but merely said: 'Dear me, what was the trouble this time, Arthur?'

'It's not Arthur, it's David.'

II

Bel turned round in surprise. She regretted the darning-basket a little. David and darning, she felt, didn't quite go together. But it was too late to put it away and take up her embroidery.

19

'Oh, David, come in! I'm glad to see you. Arthur's downstairs in the library having his evening ruined with some church squabble.'

'He's too conscientious.'

'That's what I say.'

David settled himself on the chair Bel had hoped to see her husband occupy. She was genuinely pleased to see him, though she wondered that he should come thus unannounced on a Saturday evening. For David's bachelor existence was full. But something was worrying him. She knew the signs.

'Well, David?'

David looked about him. The pleasant, richly furnished drawing-room. The stacked-up, flaming fire. The handsome, fair-haired woman opposite him, who was giving the whole a core of agreeable femininity. Here was the sympathy for which he had come.

'I thought I would look in to see you,' was all he found himself saying. 'I hadn't seen you for a day or two.'

Bel looked up from her work and smiled. 'You can smoke one pipeful here if you like.'

'No, thanks. I wouldn't dare to contaminate this room.'

Bel smiled again. David was sensitive and considerate.

'Phœbe and Henry have gone to the concert,' she said conversationally.

'How are they getting on?'

20

Bel looked at David. Here, perhaps, was her clue. 'What do you mean? As separate people, or as an engaged couple?'

'I suppose I mean as an engaged couple.'

Funny question for a man to ask. Any woman might ask it, of course. 'Quite well, I suppose. Have we *ever* known what Phœbe was thinking?'

David got up, put his hands in his pockets and took a pace or two in the room. 'But do you think she's happy?'

'I don't see much difference in her.' Bel wondered at this. What had prompted it? She put out another feeler. 'But I'm certain it's made all the difference to Henry, after what has happened to him this autumn.'

David thought of his friends Stephen and Henry Hayburn. The loss of their fortune in the City Bank crash, and the death of their mother.

'Yes, I dare say it's a good thing for him.' And then, after another silence: 'Do you think Phœbe is in love with him?'

'My dear David, I don't know.' Did all this somehow apply to David himself? What was his problem? He was striding up and down in a way quite unlike him, trying to ask her something.

Suddenly he stopped. 'Tell me this, Bel,' he said. 'Do you think it's better for a man to be married?'

'Of course.'

21

'But he's got to fall in love with somebody first?'

'Yes.'

'Would you say it was a lonely business later on, not being married?'

'Certainly.'

'The trouble with me is, I can't fall in love.'

'Nonsense.'

'It's true.'

Bel put down her work and sat, gazing away from him into the fire. She genuinely wanted to help him. Something had stirred him and made him very much in earnest about this. He was not just a boy. The great loneliness of the unmated had overwhelmed him, and he didn't know what to do about it. It was so difficult to help a man, to know a man's feelings.

David was attractive and lovable, but she could well believe he had never been in love. He was agile-minded, quick to discover his own reactions, and not, she guessed, more than normally sexed. He would laugh at his own little susceptibilities too quickly, refuse to take his feelings seriously. And he had far too many pleasant friendships with women; understood them too well, to be easily borne off his feet.

Still looking into the fire, she spoke. 'Are you anxious to be married, David?'

'I don't want life to slip past me.'

'You can afford to wait. Arthur was your

22

age when he married me.'

'Yes; but he knew he wanted to marry you for years before that. That makes all the difference.'

'Yes. I see what you mean.' Bel let him pace about for some moments more, then she asked: 'Do you know of anybody that you think is interested in you?'

'Interested?'

'Well, in love with you, then?'

'What a queer question to ask a man! Women don't show their feelings.'

'If a woman was in love with you, you would know. You're that kind of man. She would be clever if she hid it from you.'

'I don't know if that's a compliment.'

'I'm not trying to pay you compliments, David; I'm trying to help you.'

'There have been two or three.'

'I thought so. Is there anybody now?'

'Yes.'

'And what kind of feeling have you about her?'

'I like her. But since I've seen she was – well, like that, I've been keeping away.'

'Go back and have another look at her.' Bel took up her mending again. 'You know, David,' she said, 'there are some people who fall in love only after they're settled down and married.'

'Do you mean I'm one of them?'

'Maybe.'

'But it's very important for me to know.'

Bel did not reply at once. This was the strangest conversation she had had for a long time. She was very fond of David. He had been a very young man when she had married his brother. And of all the family, perhaps, she had stood nearest to him; nearer than his own sisters. There was a fastidiousness about him, a niceness, that had always appealed to her.

'I don't really know how you feel about this, David,' she said at length. 'How can I? Many women marry without love, and it turns out all right. They say it doesn't happen so often with men.'

'Would you risk it, if you were me?'

To give definite judgment was too much responsibility. Bel hedged. 'Go back and see your girl, anyway, David. Give your feelings a chance.'

Arthur Moorhouse's appearance brought this talk to an end, the church member having taken himself off. It was just as well, Bel felt. Confidences such as these tended to become dangerous. Arthur's wiry, vigorous presence brought things back to normal. He stood on the rug, his back to the blazing fire, warming himself.

'I want a cup of tea, Bel,' he said testily. 'I'm sick of folks and their blethers.'

III

Phœbe, followed by Henry Hayburn, jumped from the cab that had brought them to the New Public Halls in Berkeley Street. Inside, the auditorium was quickly filling with people. Bel had obtained the seats intended for herself and Arthur in the front of the gallery, half-way down the long hall. They ascended the main staircase, found their block in the steeply graded rows, and climbed down into their places. Sitting now, beside the eager, boyish young man who had but lately engaged himself to become her husband, Phœbe looked about her. Glasgow's large new concert hall was still a novelty to her. She looked with interest at the sea of seats in the area beneath her; the people finding their places over there in the gallery opposite; at those – scarcely to be distinguished, so great was the distance – who were filing up into the high gallery at the back.

Phœbe and Henry had no intense interest in music. But young people, so alive, could not fail to feel the latent excitement in the waiting audience. They consulted their programmes. They hung over the gallery, picking out acquaintances. They twisted themselves about to see who was near them.

Now the orchestra was coming in. The platform was becoming busy. The harpist was

25

plucking odd strings. One player nodded greeting to another. Musicians were placing their chairs to a nicety. The right positions for music-stands were being found. There was a constant tuning of the fiddles and their like. Wood and wind instruments emitted fragments of scales. Up at the back, the drummer was adjusting the tension of his drums. The air was filled with the sounds of preparation. Phœbe and Henry were enjoying themselves.

Sitting on Phœbe's other side, a young woman was making much fuss with herself. She was telling friends how she had studied recently with this very Julius Tausch who was to conduct his first popular Saturday concert in Scotland tonight. To enhance her own importance, she was doing her best to impress upon them what a singular man Herr Tausch was. He was a pupil of Mendelssohn, she said, and had succeeded Schumann to a musical post in Dusseldorf. Phœbe, avid of life herself, listened with interest, and envied the young woman her education abroad.

The noise of tuning stopped, as the first violin came in to take his seat. A hush of interest swept the halls. Late-comers tiptoed hurriedly to their seats. Now the side-curtains were held aside by an unseen hand and the new conductor, a heavily-bearded, shaggy-haired, energetic German, hurried in to take his place before the orchestra. For a moment he stood, acknowledging the welcoming applause; then he turned, tapped his desk with Teutonic vigour, and the concert had begun.

It was a Saturday concert, and the music was not, in everything, strictly classical. A popular overture. Next, an arrangement of tunes borrowed from many sources, entitled 'Melodious Congress', in which the leading instruments of the orchestra had solos to perform as an exhibition of their skill. To Phœbe it was entertaining enough. But, even so, she was not sorry to note that when the 'Melodious Congress' had been given, a certain Signora Lucia Reni would delight them with her singing. At least one could look at the singer's dress, wonder how young she really was, and if her hair was all her own.

Now the second piece was ended. Herr Tausch had laid down his baton, and gone beyond the curtain to return at once gallantly leading the Signora, who came, smiling and bowing with professional coquetry. As she took up her place at the front of the platform, Phœbe scrutinised her with interest. The singer looked thirty or thereabout. Her aspect was Parisian rather than Italian. Her skin was fair and Gallic, though her abundant hair was black. The white satin dress sat severely plain on the plump bust, the hourglass waist and the carefully corseted hips; it was only when it had come below the knee that, after the fashion of the day, it broke into lavish loops and frills. Her long kid-gloves added to the effect of whiteness. The only colour the Signora permitted herself was a red rose admirably set in her hair, killing any austerity in her dress, and somehow adding sparkle and gaiety to her features. A splendid concert appearance, Phœbe decided. But that was not all. Why was her face familiar?

Now Signora Reni was standing, charmingly serious, listening to the orchestra as it played the introduction to her aria. Now she was singing with a clear, trained, concert soprano's voice; filling the great space with a practised ease. No. Phœbe had seen this woman somewhere before, though she had never heard her perform. A long time ago, perhaps. This imperfect remembrance baffled and maddened her. Now the singer was bowing and smiling acknowledgment at the end of the song. Now she was going off. Still Phœbe could not place her in her mind.

She turned to her companion. 'Henry, have you ever seen that woman before?'

'No, never.'

'Doesn't she remind you of anybody?'

'No, I don't think so.'

The orchestra was playing again. Henry was no help, then. She couldn't have known her when she was a little girl in the country, could she? She had never known any Italians. Yet, she had heard that public singers often gave themselves Italian names. She turned to the programme once more. Lucia Reni. About a mile from the Laigh farm there was a farm called Greenhead. Its farmer was called Rennie. One of his daughters was called Lucy. Lucy Rennie. Lucia Reni. Now she was getting somewhere. The light was breaking. Yes, she had seen Lucy Rennie once or twice, when she was a little girl at the Laigh. Lucy Rennie had been, if she remembered aright, about the same age as her brother David. They had been schoolmates together. And she had seen the other Rennie sister and her father quite recently. She must, in part, be recognising a family likeness. She would have another look at her when she came back to sing again.

Phœbe gave her future husband a joyful dig. Henry, whose attention had been caught by the music, turned reluctantly to see her smiling in triumph.

'Henry! I've guessed who she is! She's no more Italian than I am!'

Henry responded to her joy with impatience. 'All right. You can tell me later,' he said, turning indignantly again to the music.

IV

David was still at Grosvenor Terrace when Phœbe and Henry Hayburn came back. In the light of his conversation with Bel and his

29

own preoccupations, he found himself watching the young people closely. Henry, coltish and uncouth, was quite obviously very much in love with Phœbe. There was something still schoolboyish in his attitude towards her; although he was twenty-three and Phœbe eighteen, he seemed very much the younger of the two. Towards Henry, Phœbe, as usual, betrayed nothing. She was cool and friendly. Nothing more. Perhaps Moorhouses were not like other people, David pondered.

'Well, children,' Bel was saying, 'did you enjoy yourselves? What about the singer?'

Phœbe turned to Arthur and David. 'Do you know who the grand new singer was?'

Arthur looked at his youngest sister with fatherly benevolence.

'Don't ask me, my dear. I don't know about these kind of people.'

'Does the name Lucia Reni sound like anybody you know?'

'It sounds to me kind o' Italian or something.'

Phœbe's eyes shone with triumph. 'It was Lucy Rennie of Greenhead!'

'Do you mean to tell me that? Old Tom Rennie's daughter?'

'Yes.'

All this was Greek to Bel. Who was Lucy Rennie? Where or what was Greenhead? Why the surprise? She asked questions.

Greenhead, it was explained to Bel, was a neighbouring farm to the Laigh. This prima donna with an Italian name was none other than the neighbouring farmer's daughter. The Moorhouse boys and Phœbe had known her family all their lives.

'I knew one of the Greenhead lassies had gone to London. She would have been better to stay at home,' Arthur said presently. The Moorhouse roots went deep into the Lowland peasantry. And, like most peasants, they were suspicious of artists and their like – seers of visions and dreamers of dreams. If you had made your fortune, walking all the while in due fear of the Lord, then perhaps you might spend some of it in buying their books or their pictures, or even in watching their performances on stages or platforms. But there contact must end.

Phœbe and David took Arthur's meaning perfectly. They were of his blood. But Bel was anxious to hear more of this woman.

What did she sing?

Phœbe had brought home a programme. It all looked very professional and high falutin.

Had she sung well?

Phœbe and Henry thought so. She had made a success and been recalled several times.

What did she look like?

She was elegantly dressed in white, and

seemed pretty in the distance.

'She'll be thirty if she's a day,' was Arthur's comment.

Bel sensed the hostility in his voice and was at a loss to account for it. Arthur was usually so fair-minded. She could not understand that, in addition to his inborn dislike of artists, he had struck upon an old family rivalry. There had been courtesy and even help between the farms, as is necessary among those who must close the ranks every now and then in their battle with Nature. But the Rennies of Greenhead had always been sharp and opportunist; while the Moorhouses of the Laigh Farm had been plodding and industrious. Now a Rennie, true to her type, had appeared and scored a point in a most unexpected and, to Arthur's thinking, none too admirable a way. And, little as it concerned him, Arthur didn't like it.

Chapter Three

If there had been a woman in the office of Arthur Moorhouse and Company, she would have noticed the difference in David's appearance at once. But these were not yet the days when women clerks were to be found everywhere. Arthur would strongly have disapproved of the idea. He had said often enough that the Candleriggs was no place for a woman. By which he meant that it was no place for a woman who was unused to the coarse oaths and obscene badinage of the carters and warehousemen as they loaded and unloaded their heavy goods, or roughly elbowed their way in this narrow, straw-and-paper-littered street where the distribution of Glasgow's food-stuffs took place.

But as it was, all the hands being male, none of them noticed that Mr. David was more meticulously dressed than usual. His old office coat was put on, of course, when he came in of a morning, but the one he hung up on the peg behind the counting-house door was new, and before he put it on again to go out it was brushed with the office clothes-brush. His waistcoat, his linen and his trousers, always careful, were even more careful these days.

In other words, David had made up his mind, and – never at any time averse to a little forethought – was laying his plans. Bel had told him to have a look at this girl again, and he had made up his mind to do so. But, careful and practised bachelor as he was, he was quite determined that this meeting should not seem deliberate. It must look casual, at all hazards. There was nothing for it, then, but to wait for an encounter. David knew the movements of his world. The chance would not long be delayed, if he put himself in the way.

It was a late November morning, bright and sparkling, with the first touches of frost. The sun, striking for a time down the narrow canyon of the Candleriggs, lent even this humdrum street a passing glory. A morning for everybody to be out. David turned back into the darkness of the warehouse. He had tried Buchanan Street several times. He would try it again, making some excuse for half an hour of escape.

He guessed, as he turned into it, that it would be full of carriages. Women of consequence would have come into town to shop. He was right. There were equipages from the West End and the country. Most of them were halted by the kerb on either side of the broad, handsome street. Cockaded flunkeys stood by impatient, high-bred horses, holding their heads or adjusting their rugs, while their stylish mistresses made their purchases, gazed at their leisure at the windows, or merely walked and talked with each other, enjoying the sunshine.

David was preparing, not for the first time, to make a detailed examination of the carriages and their occupants, when his arm was caught and firmly held by an elderly man.

'Hullo, Moorhouse. Are ye looking for somebody? Ye haven't seen my wife and girl, have ye?'

'Oh, good morning, Mr. Dermott.'

Old Robert Dermott wondered why David changed colour. 'They should be here, somewhere. They were coming in, if it was a fine morning.' It would have surprised him to know that the young man he was good-naturedly holding was there to look for them, too. They stood looking about them for some moments.

David Moorhouse, the farmer's son from Ayrshire, was not sorry to be seen thus affectionately held by one of the princes of Glasgow's shipping world – a prince who, like so many of his kind, had begun life with nothing. Nearly fifty years before, the young highland giant, who was Robert Dermott, had come to a rapidly expanding Glasgow. Now he owned a fleet of merchant-men and a house in the country overlooking a deepened Clyde. From his windows he could watch his great steamers, as they moved carefully in the narrow waterway; arriving from, or setting out for, the other side of the world.

David looked up at the grand old man beside him. As he stood there, he seemed to dominate his surroundings. There was something patriarchal about his flowing beard and his bushy eyebrows. The eyes beneath them were arrestingly gentle in all this ruggedness, as they ranged the street

35

looking for their own.

'By the way,' he said conversationally, 'I've taken somebody you know into Dermott Ships Limited. Young Stephen Hayburn. I don't know what he has got in him, but I am doing it for his father's sake. His father was a friend of mine. We learnt our ABC from the same dominie at Ardfinnan.'

David found himself saying that it was kind of Mr. Dermott.

'Kind? It's not kind if the boy has got anything in him. I hear the young one is to marry yer sister.'

'Yes, they—'

But Mr. Dermott's thoughts, still running in their own groove, went on aloud, 'Terrible smash that City Bank business. Ye know, Moorhouse, the amount of poverty and destitution up and down the country, and in this City of Glasgow this winter—'

But the amount of poverty and destitution did not at this moment prevent a particularly handsome carriage and pair making its way round from Argyle Street into Buchanan Street, the stepping horses shining with moisture after their long run into town from the country. The carriage was dark green, as was the livery of the men up in front. There were discreet monograms 'R.D.' in yellow on the doors.

Robert Dermott opened his giant's throat and bellowed: 'Here, MacDonald, stop!'

People turned round to look. The nearest horses waiting by the kerb threw up excited heads and had to be controlled. But those in the carriage in mid-stream, for whom it had been intended, had heard, too. The footman turned to tell the coachman. Two ladies were seen to lean forward and look about them. The pace slackened, and in a few moments more the horses were standing, steaming in the crisp, frosty air.

Robert Dermott, still holding David's arm, marched him forward. 'Here's the wife and Grace,' he said, beaming with pleasure. 'Come and say hullo.'

No, David pondered, as he moved forward, the thing could not have been more suitably accomplished, nor with a more casual seeming.

II

The footman was handing the ladies from the carriage. Grace Dermott sprang out first. She was a slim, fair young woman of nearer thirty than twenty. Her mother was large and commanding like her father, and some ten years younger than he. She greeted David warmly in a loud, West of Scotland voice. People turned in the street and said 'Oh, there was Mrs. Robert Dermott.' Her daughter, too, gave David her hand.

37

'Well, Mr. Moorhouse, we haven't seen you for a long time. Where have you been?'

David told Mrs. Dermott he had been busy. As he stood talking he found himself watching Grace. She was pleased to see him, but, quick to go on the defensive, he wondered now if there was more than that. He thought so. Indeed, it was to see these signs that he had put himself in her way.

In the sunshine, they walked up the street together. The horses, over-warm, had been driven on, for they must not stand in the cold. David, although he had been the guest of the Dermotts a number of times, looked at them anew this morning.

He liked them. They were effusive and kind, with that easy, enveloping kindness of simple people who had become very rich. The world had treated them well. Robert Dermott's days of striving were so far behind him that, although he talked much of his boyhood and his struggles in a bragging, old man's way, prosperity and ease had long since wiped out their bitter reality from his mind.

David's friend Stephen Hayburn had first taken him to visit them. They had accepted him at once as Stephen's friend.

He was walking between the two women. They talked of Stephen.

'Mr. Dermott has just told me that he has taken him into Dermott Ships Limited,'

David said.

'Yes, Robert felt he ought to, Mr. Moorhouse. His father was an old friend. We felt it was the least we could do,' Mrs. Dermott said. She spoke as though nobody had any reason to be uncomfortable; but if there was any difficulty, they, the powerful and benevolent Dermotts, would see to it.

'I hear that Henry Hayburn is to marry your sister, Mr. Moorhouse,' Grace said.

'Yes.'

'Is she like you to look at?'

'Not in the least.'

Mrs. Dermott laughed. 'I nearly said what a pity.'

David acknowledged the compliment and held out his hand. 'Look here, it's time I was getting back to work. I'm not as idle as I look, you know.' This last was aimed at Robert Dermott. Shipping princes did not approve of young men who appeared to have nothing to do.

'Can't we arrange for you to come and see us soon, Mr. Moorhouse?' Mrs. Dermott said. 'What about Saturday. There are trains at all kinds of times. Or perhaps it's asking too much?'

No, it was not asking too much of Mr. Moorhouse. He was merely, indeed, receiving what he had come for. 'Go back and have another look at her.' Bel's words came into his mind as he turned across Exchange

Square making for Arthur Moorhouse and Company. Grace Dermott was a handsome girl, and everything that was good. He would go and have a look at her as he had been told to.

He liked her. Without knowing it, David slackened his brisk townsman's pace, and sauntered slowly along the pavement thinking. Obviously Mrs. Dermott wanted him to come. What did Grace feel about him? Was he perhaps, after all, imagining that she loved him? But then, Bel had said he was the kind of man who would know. David thought he knew.

III

When they had finished their business, Grace Dermott and her mother ate their roast beef before the fire, in the comfortable, well-padded dining-room of one of the many hotels in George's Square. Her father, having gone back to his office for an hour, had joined them. Although they had seen each other at breakfast and were to meet again in the evening, this affectionate trio were pleased to eat their midday meal together. None of them spoke much. Robert Dermott sat enjoying vast quantities of beef, potatoes and cabbage, his glass of claret, the prosperous looks of his wife and daughter, and the blazing fire. These immediate things occupied his mind. His thoughts, for the moment, dwelt neither upon the state of British shipping, nor upon the young man they had chanced to meet this morning.

Mrs. Dermott, having attended a committee formed to relieve the present distress in the city, sat nursing her annoyance over a decision that had been taken against her wishes.

Grace alone thought of their meeting with David.

Early in the afternoon the carriage came to fetch them home. It would take them over an hour to get there. In the yellow November sunshine they took their way along the road that follows the Clyde to Dumbarton. It was getting colder. Already a thin fog was rising from the river, rising to meet the sun hanging low and wintry in the sky, turning it to a luminous disc of pale gold. The misty smoke and the tenements of Glasgow, caught in the light, made a magic of their own.

Snug among their wrappings, the Dermotts discussed their day. The provoking Distress Committee. Grace's visit to a dressmaker. The fine gold watch that had been dropped so unaccountably, that the man had said would be so difficult to mend. A new design for embroidery. The talk of those whose business it is to spend, to be pleased and receive respect wherever they may go. But presently, lulled by the beauty of the evening, the steady trot of the horses, and springing rhythm of the carriage, they sat back saying nothing more.

They were passing Kelvingrove, with the new, ornate University towering high on the hill above it. The green slopes of the park and the clumps of bare trees were lit by the dying sunshine. From the River Kelvin, too, a white mist was rising.

So her mother had asked him to pay them another visit. Grace was glad. She would see him again. At the same time she was afraid. Would the visit merely bore him? Caught up suddenly in the upsurge of her feelings she found herself twisting her gloved fingers together under the great fur rug. She knew quite well why her mother had invited David. No confidences about him had ever passed between them. But there are a great many things that women do not need to tell each other. They were passing through the village of Partick – now a busy, industrial suburb. Here and there they caught glimpses of the Clyde's busy waterway; of fussy river steamers belching smoke and churning the water with their paddles; of the many high masts of the clippers. Across the water a great iron hull stood uncompleted in the stacks, black against the sun.

If he had wanted her he would have come on his own account. He wouldn't have waited to be asked. Men were like that. They didn't need encouragement. There would be someone else. Why had her mother bothered him? They would lose dignity over this. She would tell her she did not want to see him. No. That would be absurd.

Now they were driving between farmlands. Fields of green pasturage and yellow stubble spreading over the flanks of rolling hills or stretching flatly towards the river.

But Grace, as she sat forward clasping her fingers, did not see what was around her. She saw the face of David Moorhouse, handsome, serious and, somehow, remote. And again she saw it as it was when, some weeks ago, he had bent down to pick up some trifle she had dropped on the harness-room floor, flushed and laughing, with a thick strand of chestnut hair over his brow. A woman never should give her heart until she was asked for it. She could not help herself. It had happened like that, and there was nothing to be done.

A sudden glimpse revealed the widening river in the sunset, a sheet of angry copper. Presently they had turned from the main road, passed a gatehouse and were between the trees of their own drive.

Mrs. Dermott looked at her daughter. She saw that her eyes were full of tears.

Chapter Four

Little Arthur Moorhouse had had his hair cut. And by way of recompense for stern self-control during the cutting, he had received his reward. The barber had given him a balloon. Now the seven-year-old stalwart, one hand in his mother's, the other grasping the string of his prize, was being towed about Hillhead, while Bel did her weekend shopping. Progress was not easy; for everybody else was out, on this, the last Saturday morning of November; and, as Arthur refused to look in front of him, but kept his head turned round watching the large, sea-green sphere that floated behind him, he was continually colliding with other little boys or their mothers; much to the annoyance of his own.

'Come on, dear; you can play as much as you like with your balloon when you get home.'

'Mother, would it be very unselfish of me if I gave this balloon to Tom when I get home?'

'Very.'

'Too unselfish?' Should one ever do so much for a brother? Bel looked at her son's troubled face and laughed. 'Tom's very wee, he's only three. Perhaps he would just burst it.'

'Yes; I think perhaps it would be wiser not to give it to him.'

Arthur now looked pleased and comfortable.

For a moment Bel was stricken. Was she teaching her elder son to be selfish? But really, with her mind so full of tomorrow's roast beef, and fish for tonight, and the baker and the florist, child psychology (although it was not yet known to her by that name) was too much for her this morning.

'I've not spent my Saturday penny yet,' Arthur said, suddenly stopping dead and refusing to move.

'Well, come on, dear; you'll have time to do that if we hurry. Don't dawdle.'

Arthur trotted along, meditating deeply. Now here prestige was involved. If he had only his own tastes to consider, he would buy Slim-Jim, or broken chocolates – you got a lot of that. But, on the other hand, as a man of the world and a Kelvinside Academy scholar of some three-months' standing, perhaps he owed it to himself to buy liquorice straps. The boy who arrived on Monday morning with straps of liquorice was popular and important. You flogged all the dirty, perspiring paws of your friends with the liquorice, then gave them torn-off pieces of it to eat in return for having

45

unflinchingly allowed this sadism. No. On the whole, liquorice straps would be best. He would give them to his Aunt Phœbe to keep until Monday morning. Otherwise infirmity of purpose might overcome him, and he would eat them before they could be used to increase his glory.

So in the sweetie-shop Arthur bought his liquorice. And, as she happened to be on the spot, his mother bought materials to keep him – and herself – contented in church on the morrow. As they left, tragedy occurred. Bel, quick and over-purposeful, shut the shop door behind her too soon. There was a loud report. She had crushed Arthur's balloon. On the pavement outside there was threatened lamentation.

'Now, remember, you're a big boy, Arthur. You know your mother didn't mean it.' Arthur was uncertain of his emotions, and had to be further reminded that the boys at school would think him a great baby if he cried about a silly thing like a burst balloon.

Using a child's very effective blackmail on his harassed but tender-hearted mother, he thought he might feel better if he were allowed to go down to Kelvinbridge and look down at the water rushing over the weir. Bel was not strong enough to refuse him.

II

Arthur cheered up as his mother held him to look over the parapet at the rushing Kelvin beneath him. There were great moving islands of foam and autumn leaves. He even recovered enough to spit several times and watch the result descending.

'Come along, Arthur; we really must go.' She had him on the pavement again, and was striking the dust of the parapet from him, when she came face to face with Sophia Butter, accompanied by a young woman.

'Bel, dear! And Arthur!' Sophia always made a great deal of noise about nothing. 'And look who I've got with me! Of course, you don't know her, because, of course, you haven't met. This is Lucy Rennie! This is Arthur's wife Bel!'

Bel turned to the young woman with interest. Fashionable herself, she took in her appearance at a glance. So this was the singer they had been discussing the other evening!

Miss Rennie was small, dark, rather plump and very well dressed. There was a quickness and sparkle about her manner that might have belonged to a Frenchwoman.

'I used to know your husband, Mrs. Moorhouse, although I knew David better.' She was a little affected; but that too, Bel thought, was charming. Her speech held no

47

trace of Scotch.

Bel couldn't help being interested. The very fact that Arthur disapproved of her gave her a tang. She seemed a harmless enough sort of young woman.

Sophia had never stopped chattering. 'It's too silly! I met Lucy wandering about in Hillhead. And I knew her at once after all these years! Not a bit different! Terribly smart, of course. And very grand! That's what comes of being so much in London. I am taking her in to have a cup of tea and tell me all about herself. Come along too, Bel. And Arthur will see the children – at least, if they're there. They're so awful, I never know where they are.'

It was not often that Bel went to Sophia's house. First, because she was seldom invited; and second, because its untidiness embarrassed her. Like many very orderly people, the untidiness of others made her ill at ease. But now, busy though she was, she could not refuse.

They crossed to the east side of the bridge. A few steps more took them to Rosebery Terrace. Sophia's house smelt of cooking. The little maid, who let them in, glided off in carpet slippers to get them tea. Seated in the back parlour, Bel could hear cups being indignantly banged on a tray. There was a quarrel going on between the son and daughter of the house somewhere upstairs.

48

Sophia poked up the fire. 'I think I hear the children,' she said. 'Come with me, Arthur, and we'll go and look for them. I won't be a minute. But they must be told Arthur's here. I would never hear the end of it if they didn't see him.' And Sophia went out of the room, leaving Bel and Miss Rennie altogether.

'Oh, I know Sophia of old!' Lucy Rennie said. 'She was always terribly kind.' She laughed. Gaily and intimately. As one woman of fashion to another. She gave Bel the impression that she had stopped herself just in time. That the adverb 'terribly' had been intended to qualify some adjective quite other than 'kind'. 'Funny' perhaps, or 'idiotic'.

Bel was delighted with her. Everything about Miss Rennie appealed to her. Her alertness. Her knowledge of the world. Her 'English' accent. Her poise.

'I can't believe you came from the farm next to my father-in-law's.'

'Why?'

'You don't strike me at all as being a farmer's daughter.'

Lucy smiled. 'I dare say. I have been in London for the last eight or nine years. It's a long story, but a simple one, really. Someone heard me singing when I was twenty, and offered to give me a year's training. I accepted. Soon I did some teaching, myself, to keep me going, then I began to get engagements as well as teaching. And here I am.'

'Wasn't it very hard?' Bel asked innocently.

'Abominably.'

'Weren't you very lonely?'

'Very – at first. Later I made friends, of course.' Miss Rennie allowed her eyes to twinkle. 'I'm a self-made woman, I'm afraid, Mrs. Moorhouse.'

For a moment Bel sensed that she was merely presenting her with a façade. That a quite different person might be there behind this charm. No young girl that she knew would have the hardihood to do what Miss Rennie had done. She had, surely, taken great risks. And yet Bel liked her none the less. She saw no reason to question what Lucy Rennie had told her, nor did she stop to think that this might not be quite the whole story.

'Is your home in London?'

'Yes. I have nearly all my work there. I do a certain amount of public singing, but most of my engagements are private.'

'Private?'

'Yes. People with handles to their names, and so on, give musical parties and pay me to sing at them.'

III

Further talk was interrupted by Wil Butter, a large, gawky, good-natured boy of fifteen, who burst into the room carrying Arthur pick-a-back, and followed by Margy, his sister, a long-legged girl in a pinafore. Arthur was screaming, delighted and hysterical. It was not every day that he had large cousins devoting themselves to his amusement.

Sophia followed them. 'Children, shake hands with Miss Rennie and your Auntie Bel, then go away at once. We can't hear ourselves speaking. Here's tea. No, children, you're not to eat the biscuits. They're for the visitors. Arthur, you have one, dear. That's right. That's a nice one. Wil, Margy, what did I say? Hand them to Miss Rennie at once. Margy, ask Jenny for the sugar. She's forgotten it. Lucy, how do you like your tea? Weak? Well, that's all right. It's pretty weak as it is. Sugar's just coming.'

As Bel watched Lucy, sitting easy and self-possessed in the midst of all this good-natured uproar, a scheme was forming itself in her mind. Smart people gave musical parties in London, did they? She wondered if she dare. It would be so very up-to-date, so very interesting. But, then, how did one go about it? And what did one pay?

'I'm sorry to say I didn't hear you sing at Mr. Tausch's concert in the New Public

51

Halls the other Saturday,' she said.

'I didn't either,' Sophia broke in, or, rather, deflected the ceaseless stream of her talk in their direction. 'William, my husband, and I meant to go. Then I can't remember what it was kept us. Anyway, a lady in the church told us you were just wonderful. She said you brought tears to her eyes. Now – what was it you sang she said was so beautiful? Anyway, she said she had never been so touched by singing in her life!'

Miss Rennie smiled. Even this flattering nonsense was grist to her mill. She sang for her bread-and-butter. And it did her self-esteem no harm to know that even that kind of person liked her work.

Would she be singing in Glasgow again? Bel asked. Not in the meantime. But she was in private rooms for a week or two, using the City as a centre. There was a piano where she could work, and give odd lessons. Thereafter, she was going back to Ayrshire to spend New Year with her family.

Bel rose to go. Sophia went to find Arthur for her. He had been carried off again by the larger children. Miss Rennie said she must go, too. She would leave with them.

As they said goodbye to the Butter family, Bel's mind was working. Should she ask this woman to her house? Arthur seemed to object to the entire Rennie clan, but that was ridiculous. After all, she had met this woman at his sister's. She was interesting, clever and different. Why be stodgy?

'You must come and see me, Miss Rennie,' she said as they stood at the end of the little terrace.

'I should like to.' Mrs. Arthur Moorhouse, after all, looked a woman of some consequence.

IV

A little group of ragged children, wheeling a dirty baby in a soap-box, scuttled past them. A white-faced mite, who looked two or three, but had the sharpness of six or seven, detached himself from them and held out a filthy paw to the ladies.

'Gie's a ha'penny.' His black eyes were pitiful in his little sharp face.

The ready emotion of a performing artist brought tears to Miss Rennie's eye. She drew her purse from her muff and gave him a sixpence.

Bel, not to be outdone, gave Arthur the same to give to the urchin.

'Poor little things!' Lucy Rennie said, as she watched the child scamper back to the others.

'My husband says there's terrible distress among these people this winter, Miss Rennie. There are subscriptions and charities being organised for them everywhere.'

'It's bad in London, too. I've sung at one or two charity evenings.' She looked after the ragged children. 'If you have a large drawing-room, Mrs. Moorhouse, I should be glad to do it for you. It's quite a good way to raise money.'

Bel was enchanted. But she must go warily. After all, there was Arthur.

'It would be wonderful, Miss Rennie. Come and see me next week, and meanwhile I'll discuss it with my husband. There is nothing I'd like better.'

She fixed a day, and bade Lucy Rennie a cordial goodbye. This was amazing! And for charity! Arthur couldn't be such a bear as to refuse. He couldn't be so narrow-minded. Sometime this weekend she would await her opportunity and ask him.

'Come along, Arthur; we're going to be late.'

Arthur the Second trotted home behind a mother who was carried forward on wings of delight and determination. As he had no such wings but merely his own sturdy enough little legs to depend upon, he found it hot work.

Bel was set upon having her evening. That it be charitable, was very proper; that it be smart, was imperative.

Chapter Five

There are certain strong, elderly women who work off their energy interfering with other people. Mrs. Robert Dermott was one of these. But as her interferences were on the whole benevolent, and as, in the case of the poor at least, they were accompanied by cheques of her own signing, she seemed to make strangely few enemies. If she were not interfering in person, then she was writing letters of interference. Of such are the convenors of committees.

Mrs. Dermott wrote letters all over her large, ugly and comfortable Clydeside house. At Aucheneame, her bedroom and all the living-rooms had a desk with pen and paper waiting ready to her hand. Even in the large conservatory full of palms, maidenhair fern and chirping canaries, there was a slender bamboo table waiting to creak beneath her weight as she leant upon it writing. Her spectacle-case, attached to her person, was kept full of stamps, for, as she would have told you, she hated to have to be hunting for things.

A purposeful, though not dislikeable lady, if you could stand up to her, with much of the strength and drive belonging to her husband. It was no wonder that this couple had long ago reduced their only daughter to meekness and docility. And yet, between her letter-writing and committee-attending, and after her own fashion, Mrs. Dermott was very fond of Grace. She had been thinking about her recently, and she was worried. Grace was twenty-nine and unmarried. It was high time she was. What was wrong with the young men? She was reasonably pleasant to look at, gentle and feminine, and not half-witted. What more did young men want? What kept them away?

It had never struck Mrs. Dermott that her husband's wealth, and the crashing personalities of both of them, had tended to push suitors to a distance.

On the early evening of her return from Glasgow, Mrs. Dermott sat at the writing-desk in her bedroom sucking the end of a pen and thinking. She thought of the strained look and the tears in Grace's eyes as they had driven home that afternoon. She had noticed such symptoms before. Putting two and two together, she was almost certain that the girl loved David Moorhouse. This morning, Mrs. Dermott had asked him to visit them, just as she would have asked any young man, or indeed any pleasant person who would have been willing to come. For what was the use of all the paraphernalia of hospitality if you were inhospitable? Grace, for all her seeming passiveness, had betrayed excitement at the prospect of David's visit. She must, then, take the young man seriously, and do what was best for her daughter.

What about this David Moorhouse? What sort of person was he? He had already been four or five times in Aucheneame, and Mrs. Dermott, in so far as she had thought about him at all, had liked him.

Neither she nor her husband were highly critical. They were too intent upon themselves. They met many people, and took them as they found them. He made his friends in the business world, and she in the world of philanthropy. Like most successful public people, their friends were those who worked well with them.

But now, Mrs. Dermott pondered, it was time she found out more about this young man. She must ask Grace about him. As casually as possible, of course.

II

As she rose to find her, Grace's father came into the room.

'Hullo, Robert,' she said. 'I didn't know you were home.'

Her husband stood warming his back at the bedroom fire.

'I have been thinking about Mr. Moorhouse,' Mrs. Dermott went on, 'and I've taken an idea that Grace likes him.'

Robert Dermott merely stroked his patriarch's beard with an enormous hand and said: 'Is that the way of it?'

'He seems a nice sort of young man.'

'Aye.'

'I wish you would find out something about him, Robert.'

'I know a lot about him already. I thought things might be taking a turn that way. So I took some trouble to find out.'

'And do you mean to say you never bothered to tell me?'

'It wasna verra important.'

'Then why did you bother?'

'I bother about every young man that comes here. I've a daughter in the house.'

'She's my daughter, too, Robert.'

A smile slowly lit up Robert Dermott's eyes. 'Sir William knows him and his brother,' he said.

'And what are they?'

Dermott told his wife. Three Ayrshire farmer's sons. The eldest still a farmer, but, rather surprisingly, married into the Ayrshire county. The other two brothers, Arthur and David, were prosperous cheese merchants, who somehow managed to have the bearing of professional men. Two sisters, who had made everyday marriages. And the

58

young half-sister who was engaged to Henry Hayburn.

'You seem to know all about them. You're a sly old rascal.'

'D'you want your lassie to get married to a cheese merchant?'

'Yes. If it's going to break her heart if she doesn't, Robert.'

Dermott turned and looked into the fire. 'You took me. I was only the son of a herd.'

Mrs. Dermott rose and kissed her husband – an indulgence she did not often permit herself. The Dermott's were built on a scale too imposing somehow to do much kissing.

A housemaid came in with gleaming copper cans steaming with hot water. She saw to the room and laid out such clothes as they might want for the evening. And as he stood watching her, Robert Dermott thought of a cottage fifty years ago, where the peat smoke had found its way out through a hole in the thatch. It was a far journey from there to here, but he had made it. He was not the only one who had made this journey – and with dignity – in Victorian Glasgow.

III

It would seem an impertinence that a young man, situated as David Moorhouse was, should coolly plan a visit to the only daughter of a shipping prince, to find out if he could possibly like her enough to ask her to marry him. That was the exact purpose of this visit he had arranged for himself. And yet to state it thus is somehow to misstate it. For the worldly aspect of an alliance with Grace Dermott did not greatly influence him.

David Moorhouse belonged to a rising family. But none of them were narrowly mercenary. Each and all of them had a fundamental, peasant dignity. If David had come to visit Grace, it was to seek the answer to a question that he was earnestly putting to himself. Trimmings had little to do with it. In no way could he be called contemptible. He was handsome. He was quite straight-forwardly kind. He had good manners, and a certain fastidiousness. He was quick to adapt himself to the ways of those about him, because he had been born sensitive. In other words, he was socially adroit. He must not be labelled a common schemer. There was nothing of that about him.

And yet it was a very collected sort of young man who gave his name to the man-servant that winter afternoon at the door of Aucheneame. He had a complete hold of his emotions, for the good reason that he had no strong emotions to take hold of. And when, some moments later, he stood in the open doorway of Mrs. Dermott's drawing-room

60

and caught a glimpse in a mirror of himself standing with a smile on his face, ready to be welcomed by his hostess, the elegant cut of his frock-coat and trousers reassured him. He would be able to give his usual easy performance, and from behind that, he hoped to be able to make up his mind.

Grace and her mother were in the room. Mrs. Dermott, advancing upon him in a way that was somehow reminiscent of one of her husband's ocean-going steamers, conducted him to a chair by a heaped-up fire, speaking at the same time words of welcome, regret at the coldness of the day, and assurances that tea would be here immediately, all in her loud, assured voice.

Grace's colour had risen and her eyes were shining. Surely he had guessed aright her feeling for him. It was for him now to search for his own.

It was bleak outside the large windows, but the bright leaping fire seemed to gather the little party into its friendly glow. Darkness was falling quickly now, but the shadows, as they deepened in the great tasteless room, merely served to make their circle more friendly.

Tea came, and the master of the house was called. The Dermotts could not help themselves. Their warm-heartedness towards each other was easily extended to take in their guest. If they had had no deeper interest, if he had merely been a passing visitor, it would have been much the same. Grace's parents had much to say. He could sit, eat his buttered toast and observe. Grace seemed quite unembarrassed. She poured out tea and looked after everybody, smiling indulgently at him as one young person to another, when the talkativeness of her parents clashed; or when, as happened frequently in their vitality and enthusiasm, they fell into argument with each other.

David, trying to be pleased, assured himself that she was more appealing than he had ever known her.

'Are you very anxious to be married?'

'I don't want life to slip past me.'

His conversation with Bel. He was honestly seeking the answer. Could this gentle young woman hold on to life for him? Keep it from slipping past him? Allow it to unroll itself richly and naturally before him? Prevent it from drifting on to the end, arid and aimless, a thing of unsatisfied instincts, a barren passing of the time? David was beginning to think so.

He felt happy and at ease. If Grace really wanted it, her parents, surely, would not make it difficult. She was not in her first youth. Marriage might easily miss her now. Rightly he guessed that the way would be made plain for him to find his place as the prince consort in this shipping dynasty.

The fine china and solid silver were being removed, blinds were pulled down, curtains drawn. Robert Dermott had gone off to see to some business. His wife rose.

'You will stay for a meal tonight, Mr. Moorhouse? It's nice to have you all to ourselves.'

David was pleased to accept.

'I have a letter to go to the post, if you'll excuse me. You must just try to put up with Grace by herself for a little. Do you mind?'

No, David didn't mind. So they were throwing her deliberately in his way, were they. Very well. So much the better.

IV

Grace Dermott had repose of manner. Perhaps it came from having to live with stormy, energetic parents, having to keep calm in the centre of the turmoil they created around her. This quality stood her in good stead. Even now, when the storm raged in her own senses, she continued to seem at peace.

Left alone with David, she rose, stirred the fire, and bade him take the great chair that her father had quitted, regretting the while that it was grown too dark and cold to be outside.

David, too, seemed at his ease. In this atmosphere the couple talked. Of trivialities. Of the terrier lying on the rug in front of the

63

fire. Of the people they knew. Of books. Of recent visits to the theatre. Of themselves. Of what does any civilised man or woman talk, when the battle of sex is being fought out between them? Any talk is a revealing of the one to the other. Its subject does not matter.

Grace's sensibilities were not any less quick than those of the young man who sat before her. Like herself, he was restrained and friendly. They had let themselves fall into a pleasant adult intimacy. There was no callow boy-and-girl self-consciousness. Yet each was intensely conscious of the other.

She had no doubts about herself. If this young man who was bending forward, his face aglow in the firelight, wanted her, she was his for the taking. Quite ridiculous things moved her. A way he had of putting back his thick chestnut hair. The set of his mouth and eyes when he smiled. Certain inflections of his voice. In other words, she was prepared to adore David Moorhouse in the most normal way possible.

But when she came to try to read his mind towards herself, Grace was baffled. As his good-mannered talk flowed on, she was puzzled. What had brought him here? Love for herself? She had no idea. She could find goodwill, pleasure in her company, a sincere attempt to make himself attractive to her. But further than that she could not yet penetrate. Suppose he were thrown thus

64

intimately together with any other young woman? Would he behave in the same good-mannered way? She could not tell.

Meanwhile she must be glad she had him by her; take what she could from this hour; encourage him, in so far as dignity would permit, to visit her again.

Grace sat late before her bedroom fire that night. She was not unhappy. At parting he had given her his hand and asked if he might come soon again. It might be difficult to guess his feelings, but in doing this he had, at least, given a sign.

Chapter Six

Arthur Moorhouse saw his foreman turn the key in the main door of Arthur Moorhouse and Company. 'I'll go up to the Infirmary myself, James, and I'll meet you at the Cross at three.' He turned in the direction of the Traders' Club. He was glad to find the sombre dining-room empty, though indeed he had expected this, for most members ate their midday-meal at home on Saturdays, or snatched food quickly elsewhere before they went to golf – a game which, at this time, was beginning to be fashionable. He sat at a table by himself, glad to eat his chop in peace. It had been a distressing morning. There had been an accident to one of his packers.

The man was a raw Highland crofter, who, like so many of his kind, had been driven to the City to make a living. A startled dray-horse had suddenly backed, and a wheel had passed over his foot. Arthur had seen the man and his foot before they had been able to have him taken to hospital. It had been a sickening and pitiful sight. As he sat waiting, numb and patient, afraid to stir lest he increase his pain, the Highlander had reminded Arthur of a wild thing in a trap.

'Have ye a wife, McCrimmon?'

'Aye.'

'And weans?'

'Aye.'

'I'll go and see yer wife and take yer wages to her.'

Tears rolled down the man's cheeks. That had been thanks enough for Arthur. After his meal he took himself up the hill to the Royal Infirmary, and was told that the foot had been amputated. Sorrowful, he turned from the door, and made his way down towards the Cross to break the news to the man's wife and give her a week's wages.

Arthur had arranged with his foreman to meet him; for this part of the city, small in area, yet with more than one-quarter of its inhabitants thrust together into its stews and slums, was a labyrinth to anyone who did not know it. The High Street was waking up to its usual Saturday orgy. Hungry, barefoot children, drink-sodden men and women, tired and struggling humanity. The dark side of this great, successful city. Arthur was well used to the look of these people. As a rule he accepted them, telling himself, as all his like did, that do what one would, poverty and squalor would always be. But today the sights about him weighed upon him more heavily. There were plans, he knew – plans and passionate appeals on behalf of the victims of this slumdom. But even if they bore fruit this afternoon, they would be too late to save that consumptive drab, that little group of undernourished children. He hurried on, comforting his conscience with a promise to give as much as he could to charity.

His foreman was waiting for him. Together they set off down one of the nearby wynds. He was glad to have protection. For, as the man knew this region of 'ticketed houses', and had, indeed, been to the injured man's quarters, he was able to show the way. No easy matter. For in this part of the town a policeman, tracking a criminal, would receive such an address as: 'Crawford's Wynd, No. 21, Back Land, stair second on left, three up, left lobby facing the door.' Such directions were keys of labyrinths – labyrinths of crime and disease, indecency and death. Arthur followed through a filthy entrance, across another narrow wynd, up stairs rank with humanity, and along a passage where they had to strike matches to see their way. Everywhere they were followed by eyes – dull eyes, over-bright eyes, pitiful eyes, bewildered, childish eyes; the eyes of those to whom the great revolution of the nineteenth century, the triumph of iron ships, the expansion of industry, had been cruel.

Their luck was in. They found Mc-Crimmon's wife at home. That is, if a part of a room partitioned off by thin wood can be called home. A low fire was burning, and by its light and such as came through the small window, Arthur saw a young woman and two little children. From what he had seen of the denizens of this place on his way up, he was surprised that the woman was normally tall. Though she was pale, she was neither ailing nor wasted. There were two chairs, a table and even a bed. An attempt was made at cleanliness – a difficult feat this, where water had to be fetched up several flights of stairs.

The sight of the black-coated gentleman threw the woman into a dumb agitation. It could forebode nothing but trouble. She stood in the middle of the room, her children clutching her dress, waiting for Arthur to speak.

'Are you Mrs. McCrimmon?' he asked.

'Yes, sir. Mrs. McCrimmon. Hamish Mc-

Crimmon's wife. Are you being Mr. Moor-house?'

'Yes.'

'I was after seeing you before once in the distance, sir.' She twisted her rough apron in her hands. Her voice had the soft beauty of the north. She spoke carefully, this English language that she had learnt. Arthur was moved by her dignity – a peasant dignity, that any Moorhouse could well understand.

'I brought yer man's wages, Mrs. Mc-Crimmon,' he said.

'Oh, thank you, sir.' She took the envelope, and looked about her, as though she were looking for the answer to some question in the dark corners of the room.

'Yer man's had an accident, Mrs. Mc-Crimmon.' Arthur had to force the words out of himself.

'An accident?'

'Sit down at the table and I'll tell ye.'

The woman went rigid. A more imaginative visitor than Arthur Moorhouse might have guessed that she was drawing on the immense reserve of pride that was her birth-right. 'I'll be standing where I am, Mr. Moorhouse, please.'

'A wheel went over his foot. They had to take it off at the Royal Infirmary this afternoon.'

She stood, still saying nothing. The fingers of each hand kept moving in the hair of the two infants that clung to her. That was all.

Arthur did not fully comprehend that the dry eyes were staring straight into the face of starvation, but his robust companion knew.

There was nothing to be done but go on stammering out details: what they had said at the hospital; when she might see him if she went. The woman stood saying nothing.

If she had lost control and screamed, as indeed they could even now hear a drunken woman screaming in another room, it would have been pitiable. But somehow it was more than that. This woman was on a level with himself. She and these children had no right in this place. He must get her out of it to a place where there was air and light and decency. How had she and her husband come to occupy this room? How had they come to set upon themselves Glasgow's special stigma, as inhabitants of 'ticketed houses'?

But she was not to be talked to. He held out his hand. She did not seem to notice it. 'You know where my office is, Mrs. McCrimmon. If you come next Saturday morning at twelve o'clock I'll give you yer man's wages again.'

A strain seemed to go out of her face. She managed to look at him. 'If you pay me money, I'll be working for it, Mr. Moorhouse.'

Arthur foresaw a battle with her pride. He became brusque.

'Well, anyway, I've got to go now. Goodbye. And come and see me if you're in any trouble, Mrs. McCrimmon.' His sharp, purposeful tone was too much for her.

'Yes, sir. God bless you, Mr. Moorhouse.'

Arthur turned and left her, followed by his man. He was shaken by this meeting. In a voice that was still abrupt he bade him goodday, thanked him shortly for troubling to come with him, and walked off in the direction of the Kelvinside tram. His stocky foreman stood watching the lean, striding figure until it was lost in the Saturday rabble.

II

Bel wondered, as she sat at her midday meal with little Arthur and Phœbe, if it would be worthwhile to talk to her sister-in-law about the charity concert. Her enthusiasm decided her.

'I met Lucy Rennie this morning at Sophia's,' she began.

'Did you?' Phœbe went on with her soup.

For the last eight years she had had the upbringing of Phœbe, and, with very good reason, she loved her husband's youngest sister. But every now and then in these eight years Bel had been overcome with a strong

71

impulse to smack her. Why couldn't she settle down to a good gossip once in a while? Why couldn't she ask what Miss Rennie looked like at close quarters? If she was pleasant to speak to? What kind of clothes she wore? Why she was at Sophia's? How long she was to be in Glasgow? In fact, all the pleasant trivialities of normal feminine intercourse.

Bel should have known better. At more serious moments than this, Phœbe had, maddeningly, held her tongue.

'Do you remember her when you were a little girl at the Laigh Farm?' Bel persisted.

'I saw her once or twice in church.'

'Did she sing in those days?'

'I don't remember. Yes. I think she was in the choir.'

'Did she never come to the Laigh Farm?'

'I don't remember.'

No. It was too hard going with Phœbe. And yet the girl had bounced in from a concert two weeks ago to tell David and Arthur that this young lady with the Italian-sounding name of Lucia Reni was none other than Lucy Rennie of Greenhead. Yes. Phœbe was quite unaccountable.

Bel gave it up. She had been seeking some clue to the Moorhouse dislike of the Rennie's – a clue that might help her to overcome Arthur's expected resistance. But it was no use. She would have to plan the campaign by herself.

72

Arthur was brusque and businesslike, but beneath, as his wife very well knew, there was a sympathy that could be quickly touched. Before she had told him anything of Lucy Rennie and the concert, she would tell him about the ragged children. And from there she would lead through easy stages to the meeting with Miss Rennie at Sophia's, and how they had planned a drawing-room concert to help the suffering in the city. To this, Bel hoped, Arthur could not but respond.

But as she sat, later that afternoon, giving a cold and dejected husband tea, Bel wondered. Arthur had not yet told her what had kept him in the City. His mood was dark. It would be folly to trouble him now. She must have patience.

There was a real understanding between these two. In the nine years of their marriage each had learnt of the other where it was possible to lean, where to go lightly. Good-will, intelligence and a fundamental respect, each for the other, had brought together a man and a woman who were widely dis-similar. Bel saw that Arthur was preoccupied and weary. She knew that he would snap her head off if she mentioned the concert. But likewise did she know that this would pass; that this thing, whatever it was, pent up inside him, would have to be told, and told to herself as Arthur's inevitable confidante.

Arthur was therefore allowed to drink his tea in peace, and when it was done to sit on the other side of the fire from a comfortable and untroublesome wife, who seemed wholly intent upon her embroidery.

III

'Well, dear, were you busy this afternoon?' she ventured presently.

'One of the men in the warehouse got his foot smashed.'

'Our warehouse, Arthur?' Bel put her sewing in her lap.

'Aye. They took his foot off.'

'Oh! Poor thing! Do I know him?'

'No. I don't think so. His name's Hamish McCrimmon. He's from the Islands. He's just been in Glasgow a week or two.'

'Has he got a wife?'

'A wife and two weans. I had to go and tell her, poor body.'

Bel took up her work again. Here was her husband at his best. Taking responsibility upon himself. Shelving nothing that was disagreeable, merely because he didn't like it. 'Poor Arthur!' she said. 'What a thing to have to do!'

Arthur gave a grunt of self-depreciation.

'Is she Highland, too?'

'Aye.'

74

Nothing more was said for some moments. Suddenly Arthur sprang to his feet as though he had been stung. He stood on the rug in front of the fire looking down at her. 'She was in one of those terrible rooms off the Briggate. I've never seen anything like it!'

By hearsay and description Bel knew very well what these places were like. Had not her elder son at the age of three had his clothing stripped from him in some such den? Were not reformers and social workers telling those who had ears to hear what such places were like?

'Was she a slum woman, Arthur?' she asked.

'No. She seemed to me a decent Hielan' body, that didn't know where she had landed. She was like a – a bird that was taken and put in a cage.'

It was not often that Arthur took to poetry. Bel did not need to look up to realise that what he had seen had moved him to a great pity.

'What did she do when you told her, dear?'

'She just stood – stood with her bairns hanging on to her.' Arthur let his voice steady itself for a moment, then he exploded savagely, 'Dirty, stinking place!'

Bel said nothing. She merely bent her head over her work. Her own frivolous scheme had faded. Her mind was filled with the picture he had shown her.

As he stood looking indignantly about him, Arthur saw a tear fall upon her hand. Neither of them spoke for a time.

'What are you doing to help her?' Bel asked.

'I'm not sure yet. She's to come to the office next Saturday anyway and get his wages.'

'I'll come down and see her.'

'I would like if you could.' Arthur sat down again. His feelings were relieved. He had come very near to Bel. For a moment he sat thinking. 'That's a terrible place where she is,' he went on. 'It'll be the death of them. I was thinking, maybe, we could get the coach-man's house cleaned out and give it to them.'

Bel looked up. 'When the man comes out, couldn't you send them all home to the Islands?'

'He came from the Islands to get work.'

'Times are bad here, Arthur.'

'They're worse there.'

Bel had been biding her time about the coachman's house. She had been delighted when Arthur had bought a house that had one. They had been only six months in the West End, in this fine house in Grosvenor Terrace. That was expense enough for the moment. But, inevitably, if you had a coach-house, sooner or later you would have a carriage. Especially when everyone else around you had one. Unless, of course, you filled the living-quarters with lame ducks, and were unable to house a coachman. And here was Arthur suggesting they should do just that thing. There might be no getting rid of the McCrimmons. Bel and her family were of the sort that attracted hangers-on, and she knew it. Her prudence told her that they might be burdened with a useless, lame Highlander, a feckless wife, and an ever-increasing number of children, who took her charity and house-room, and thwarted her ambitions to have a smart carriage like her neighbours.

Arthur wondered at the silence his wife had fallen into. The idea of having a carriage of his own had not yet entered his mind. 'Well, my dear, do ye not think it would be the right thing to do?'

'What, Arthur?' Bel brought herself back from her own thoughts.

'The coach-house is standing there doing nothing.'

When Bel capitulated, she had the great merit of capitulating fully and handsomely. She had done it in her life before, and she made such a capitulation now.

'Of course, Arthur; we'll get the rooms cleared out and tell the poor woman to come when she can.'

'You're a good lassie,' Arthur said, looking at his wife as she rose to put away her sewing.

Bel laughed, a little emotionally. 'Yes,' she said, 'I sometimes think I am. I must go and see what the children are doing.'

And on her way upstairs to the nursery it came to her that instead of winning her difficult battle about Lucy Rennie and the concert, the war had been carried into her own territory and she had lost disastrously.

Chapter Seven

But not irretrievably.

The Lucy Rennie affair was bound to come up again. For the remainder of the day Bel was content to bask in her husband's goodwill. They were busy people. They had little enough time to water the plant of connubial tenderness. And, like a sensible woman, she knew that when it blossomed afresh, it would be vandalism to break down so delicate a blooming. She was happy to let matters be.

But on the following day things developed. Arthur had now obtained a family ticket to the Botanic Gardens – that select outdoor club of Western Glasgow. It was their custom to join the after-church parade of wealthy citizens there. They did this on fine Sundays to give themselves an appetite for their roast beef, to display Bel's smart clothes, to see and be seen.

There was a snatch of November sunshine as they took a turn or two in front of the great glass-house, watching the passers-by and greeting friends. Suddenly Bel became aware of a hand lightly laid upon her arm. She turned round to see Miss Rennie standing beside her.

'Good morning, Mrs. Moorhouse. I have just come across to ask you to introduce me to an old friend.' She smiled at Arthur.

A little flurried, Bel made the introduction. Arthur was gravely polite.

'I don't believe you remember me, Mr. Moorhouse,' she said, giving Arthur her hand.

'Aye. Fine. Many a time have I helped yer father to tie corn,' Arthur replied, kindly enough.

'I mustn't keep you,' Miss Rennie said. 'I must go back to my friends. But I just wondered if you had thought any more about a drawing-room concert, Mrs. Moorhouse?'

Bel felt caught. 'I haven't had time to discuss it properly,' she said quickly. 'But I'll let you know when you come to see me.'

With a goodbye, Miss Rennie turned and went.

'So that's old Tom Rennie's girl, is it?' Arthur said as they moved on. 'Plenty of airs and graces. And plenty of the Rennie cheek.

But how do ye know her?'

'I met her yesterday at Sophia's, Arthur. I forgot to tell you.' Forgot was perhaps not the right word, but how else was Bel to explain it?

'What's all this about coming to see you?'

She would have to tell him now. And perhaps it was all for the best that it happened so. She told Arthur of the ragged children, of Lucy Rennie's quick sympathy, and her offer to sing.

Arthur grunted, but Bel did not read discouragement from this and continued: 'She's been doing it in London. I said I would talk to you about it.' She looked at her husband. 'I feel perhaps it's our duty to help.'

'I don't like the Rennies. And I don't like public singers.'

'That's a little old-fashioned, dear. You know, we might make thirty or forty pounds.'

Arthur merely grunted once more.

But Bel was determined to have her concert. She must use whatever means came to her hand. 'No, I don't think she's bold or heartless,' she said after a moment. 'In fact it was Miss Rennie who first thought of giving money to that poor little child, Arthur. I don't think you are being quite fair, dear.'

'Maybe not, but I can't help it.'

Bel tried her final shot. 'After all, the child we gave the money to might have been one of the poor little children you saw in that terrible place.'

Arthur said nothing to this. She took it as a good sign. She tried again. 'Surely you must feel that we should do all we can, dear.'

Arthur had retreated inside himself. He looked at the crowd of well-dressed people as they milled about in the wintry sunshine, elegant, slim-waisted ladies in their furs and finery, smilingly acknowledging the greetings of frock-coated, bearded men politely raising silk hats from sleek, macassared heads. A world that was taking little heed of the tragic world that was so near them. The balance was wrong somewhere. But it was difficult, this, unless you had seen the other side of the picture for yourself. No. It would be wrong if he stopped his wife's generous impulses. A fashionable drawing-room concert did not seem a very effective way to attack the problem of the slums. But, after all, what could a nice woman do about it? Women could not leave their homes like men. Women didn't go into the world, or at least only those brazen 'New Women' did. And he had no wish for his wife to be one of these. Yes, he supposed she had better go on with it if she wanted to. She was a good girl, Bel, and had shown great understanding about the McCrimmons. But he didn't want her to be permanently mixed up with this Rennie girl.

'Is the Rennie lassie to be in Glasgow long?' he asked presently.

'No. Only for a short time,' Bel said,

anxiously trying to follow the train of his thought. 'That's why I was hoping we might decide about this at once.'

Arthur considered the matter for a step or two further. 'Well, if ye can manage it, I dare say ye had better do it,' he said.

Bel was delighted. But she knew better than to show her delight. She received her husband's permission as though he had conferred upon her a solemn mission.

'Who will ye get to help ye?' he asked.

Bel considered. 'I think I'll ask Mary,' she said, with a fine show of thoughtfulness. After all, his sister Mary was safe. None of them liked her much. But she was pious, and would give the occasion all the sanctity it needed. Besides, she was lazy, wouldn't interfere, and her husband, George Mc-Nairn, was a baillie of the City.

As she stood at her own front door waiting for her husband to find his latch-key, Bel felt uplifted. There was nothing like a walk in the Botanic Gardens to give you an appetite for roast beef.

II

Bel's relationship with her husband's married sisters was made up of some affection and much criticism. On the whole perhaps, she liked Sophia best, because, at every point, she

82

felt herself Sophia's superior: house, management of her children, personal looks – everything. And Sophia, good loquacious creature, would have been the first to admit it. Indeed, she would almost go out of her chattering way to tell Bel how well she looked, how well-run her house was, and however did she manage it? And that she, Sophia, somehow never seemed to have the time to keep herself and her possessions properly straight. She would even admit her own parsimony with an easy, flustered laugh. 'Well, perhaps William and I *were* a wee bit mean about the special collection, dear, but with growing children it takes us all our time.' No, Bel could hold Sophia in comfortable, complacent contempt, and really quite like her.

With Mary McNairn it was more difficult. She was the wife of a baillie of the City of Glasgow. Thirty-eight, still good-looking in a plump, smooth sort of way, and, Bel considered, unbearably smug. Yet Mary had her uses. Bel couldn't quite do without Mary. For Mary and her husband, the baillie, represented official Glasgow. George McNairn had, in certain directions, influence; and the presence of himself and his wife would, at least, stamp any function with respectability. And it was just this that Bel wanted now. You had to be careful of your reputation when it came to associating with women like Lucy Rennie, who had actually, she gathered, stood upon the stage of a theatre. It was Bel's ambition to be considered smart, but she abhorred the thought of being considered fast.

And so in the week following the Sunday walk in the Botanic Gardens, Bel set out upon a visit to Albany Place.

Mary was, as Bel had expected, enjoying her three o'clock tea. Enjoying was the word; for Mary saw to it that such means of enjoyment as toast dripping with butter, and cakes dripping with cream should not be wanting. The McNairns were piously thankful to Providence for making so many good things available, and they were not slow to avail themselves of them.

Mary was, on the whole, pleased to see Bel. Like most people who sit about and eat too much, she had a tendency to find life savourless at times. And this dull, early December day was one of these times. She was quite by herself. Her little twin daughters were out with the nurse-house-maid, and the boys were not yet home from school. Besides, Bel, she felt certain, was taking care of her figure, and would not sensibly reduce the supply of toast and cream sandwich intended for herself.

'Well, Bel dear,' she said in her flat, pleasant voice. 'This is a great surprise. We never see you, these days.' She presented her sister-in-law with a smooth, plump cheek.

84

Bel settled her elegant self down in Mary's snug, over-furnished little parlour. It was ridiculous for Mary to be wearing the black of middle age already. After all, she was only six years older than herself, Bel reckoned. In a calm, Madonna-like way, Mary used to be the beauty of the family. She should go for walks and eat less, and she would look as handsome as ever.

Bel drew the gloves from her well-tended hands and accepted a cup of tea. She declined a succulent slab of toast. 'No, thank you, dear. I'm not eating between meals. I read in a magazine that it's very bad for the digestion.' But seeing something that might easily be offence in Mary's eyes, and feeling her reproof had been too pointed, she changed her mind. 'Well, dear, may I have one piece?' Bel was glad to see that Mary looked happier now.

She made the proper inquiries. Mary's children, she found to her intense relief, were all much as usual. The baillie was finding his business slow on account of the bad times this autumn. But as a member of the Town Council, he was very busy and, Bel was given to understand from the tone of Mary's voice, his services were of the first importance to the welfare of the City.

Bel said what was expected of her, and agreed that George McNairn must be very busy and important indeed. She even went so far as to say she couldn't imagine how he did it all; although she was firmly convinced that her pompous, platitudinous and slow-moving brother-in-law did as little as he possibly could. Concord being established, however, she came to the reason of her visit.

'I want your advice, dear, about something,' she began. 'You see, I felt that as you and George went to so many official functions, you would be the best ones to help me.'

Mary took up a fine lace handkerchief and wiped some melted butter from her fingers. If Bel had not been there, she would have licked them. It was a pity, she reflected, to waste good butter. She would be very glad to give Bel advice. Like many people who are too inert to pursue much activity themselves, she and her husband felt fully qualified to advise in the activities of others. She indicated, absent-mindedly helping herself now to an ample slice of cream sandwich, that if there was any point upon which she could advise Bel, Bel could count upon her so doing.

'Well, dear, I suppose Sophia will have told you that Lucy Rennie, the daughter of an old neighbouring farmer of your father, has been singing in Glasgow. She became a professional singer. Wonderful, everybody says.'

'I haven't seen Sophia for a week or two. It's time she was coming to see me,' was Mary's only comment.

Bel had to stop herself from feeling annoyed. Was Mary so self-centred that she could not be stimulated by this not uninteresting piece of news? News about someone she must have known as a girl.

'Did you know Lucy Rennie?' she asked.

'Yes; we knew all the Rennies.'

And as Mary merely went on eating, Bel continued: 'Well, Arthur and I think it would be such a good idea if Miss Rennie gave a little charity concert in our drawing-room. There have been so many appeals for the poor this winter.'

Mary managed to catch some of the cream that looked like falling out at the other side of her cake by biting it just in time; then she asked: 'How much will you have to pay Lucy Rennie?'

'She's offered to do it for nothing, dear.'

Mary showed no surprise at this. She merely examined her cake to see that no more cream was eluding her. 'At least you'll need to pay a pianist,' she said.

'Even if we have to, that won't be much. Arthur would be glad to pay that. No, thanks, Mary. But I'll have some tea. So we thought, perhaps, that you and George would help. Ask some well-known people to come. George might even approach the Lord Provost. You see, if it's made important like that, you can really make something with a silver and gold collection.'

Mary swallowed the last of her slice and again applied the lace handkerchief to her plump white finger. She had no objection to doing things that made her feel important. 'I'll speak to George about it, dear. His time's very taken up just now, but he'll help if he can.'

'Miss Rennie's coming to tea tomorrow, Mary. Would you care to come and meet her?'

'No, thank you, dear. Our family never liked the Rennies.'

'I can't understand why.'

'I don't know, Bel. It's just an old feeling. You say you met her at Sophia's?'

'Yes.'

'Sophia should have let her be.'

'She seems a very bright, good-mannered young lady,' Bel insisted.

'I dare say. But I don't know. Anyway, George and I will do our duty, when you tell us what you've arranged. It's the charity that matters.'

Really, Mary was maddening, Bel reflected as she made her way home. It was as though Mary had said to her: 'We can't touch pitch ourselves, dear, but we'll do everything to help you if you want to touch it.' Oh, the smugness of these McNairns! But, for the moment, she must put up with it.

III

On the afternoon of the next day Miss Rennie paid her visit, and in doing so confirmed the good opinion Bel had formed of her. In the pleasant orderliness of her own drawing-room, Bel gave her tea, and heard her ideas concerning the evening of charitable music. A musician whose name was a household word in refined Glasgow would be her accompanist and would himself play pieces on the piano. She had, she said, persuaded him also to give his services for charity. Bel was delighted. It remained to fix the evening and the details of the entertainment. She would let Miss Rennie know.

Looking in that evening, David found Bel in high feather. She was bursting with her project. She took him aside, wanting his advice about everything. What did he think about it? Wasn't it a good idea? The McNairns were helping. They would bring some of official Glasgow. How many did he think the room would hold? Where did he think the piano ought to be? What about refreshment? What would be right and proper? David was the member of the family who went about. He must tell her. But as she talked, she began to feel a lack of enthusiasm. He seemed worried and anxious. By degrees it was borne in upon her that she was being selfish; that David had, perhaps, his own problems about which he had come for advice. Her mind went back to their last talk.

'Well, David, and have you taken the advice I gave you?' she said presently. They were in the parlour of the house. David was in front of the fire looking down upon her.

David did not answer at once, but colour came into his face.

'Have you, David?'

Again he waited a moment before he answered her. 'I wrote her a letter tonight asking her to marry me. I posted it on my way up here.'

'David!' She didn't know what to make of all this. 'David, sit down and tell me. Who is she? I don't even know that.'

'She's the daughter of old Robert Dermott of Dermott Ships. They're friends of the Hayburns.'

Of course Bel had heard of them. But how could David have made up his mind so quickly? 'Did you see her again as I said you should?'

'Yes.'

'And that settled it?'

'I think so.'

'*Think*, David? But you've just written to her to ask her to marry you!'

'Well, I'm sure of it, then.'

Strange boy. Why all this hurry? And why had he written to her? Why hadn't he gone to see her? They neither of them spoke for a

90

time. They sat, staring at the fire. Yet Bel felt she could not let it go at this.

'But, David, is it all right?' she asked at length. 'I feel that there's more to be said. You haven't rushed into this in a fit of – of, I don't know what, really – well, because she's rich, or you just want to be married or something?'

'No. I've made up my mind.'

'But are you happy about it? Will you be happy if she accepts you?'

'Yes. I'm queer, Bel. I don't think there's any getting away from that. I'm quite certain that this marriage, if it comes off, will be the making of me. You yourself told me that some people don't fall in love until they're married. I like everything about Grace Dermott. I'm taking a chance.'

They were interrupted at this moment, and Bel was grateful.

There was nothing more, she felt, that could be said.

Chapter Eight

Presently David rose, and bidding the family goodnight took himself home. It was a wet, blustery night as he walked across to his rooms in Hillhead. On the corner of his own street was the pillar-box into which he had dropped his letter of proposal. He looked at its black shape. No. There was no getting it out. He turned into his own entrance. Draughts of air, eddying in from the street, were making the gas-light flicker. The scrubbed and whitened stone staircase was unwelcoming and chill. He sat down by his fireside thinking. He had come home from his visit to Grace Dermott pleased with himself and with her. Grace had been so gentle, so sensible. He had felt warmed and uplifted. Glad to find himself thus, he had fanned the flame, putting this warmth he had felt to the front of his mind and thrusting doubts back out of sight. His self-persuasion had been successful. It had ended in the letter he had written this evening. Now that a step that might be irretrievable was taken, he was suffering from the reaction. Alarmed by this crisis of his own making, he had gone round to Bel for comfort and advice. For the first time in his life, he had not found it. Bel could do nothing but chatter about the arrangements for the charity concert she was planning. And then, when he had told her, she had been very surprised and seemed anything but sure he had done rightly. Bel was not usually so obtuse as this. She knew his difficulties. At least she might have shown some understanding.

David got up with a sigh. It had taken him

something to write that letter. He thought of the young woman he had asked to be his wife. She was superior in his mind to any other he could think of. Even without Bel's assurances, he felt he had done right.

He turned to his sitting-room table preparing to reach up, turn out the jets in the gaselier that hung above it and go to bed. On the red baize table-cloth lay a clean pad of blotting-paper. He could see it had the reverse imprint of the short letter he had written to Grace. He tore off the sheet. Should he hold it up to the mirror to read again the words he had written? On a quick impulse, he crushed up the blotting-paper and thrust it into the fire. He stood watching the flame spring up and die away, then turned back to extinguish the light. There was nothing more he could do until he had received her reply.

II

Grace did not keep him waiting. After a day's interval her answer came. It seemed to David a cool letter, telling him that she was much surprised at what she had found in his note, that he had given her no sign he had any such feelings towards her, and wouldn't he come soon and discuss the matter with her?

It was a curious thing that this young man,

who was not insensitive, should go so far astray in his assessment of her reply. Didn't Grace want him after all then, that she wanted to talk about it? Why discuss anything? What was there to discuss?

He did not see that his proposal of marriage had been accepted; that there was nothing for her to do but answer his own formal letter with a formal letter of reply; that Grace was surprised and disappointed that he should have written to her, instead of coming to her himself to make his proposal; that if she had not wanted him, she would not have asked him to come on any account.

But now this morning he must certainly go and see her. Through the good offices of his landlady he sent some excuse to Arthur for his absence from work, and set out for Aucheneame.

It was unreal somehow, this short morning journey on the empty down-river train. There was nothing remarkable about it in itself, but some of its trivial details were to remain with him. The upcoming trains bearing businessmen to the City. It seemed so unaccountable that he should be going in the opposite direction. The misty Clyde. It was high water and shipping was brisk. A grain clipper had swung across the river and was holding up the traffic. Two steam-tugs were pulling it straight. The railway carriage was cold. The warming-pan was tepid. He would always

have a picture of himself huddled into a
corner wondering what the day would bring
him.

Now he was at the station. It was some
distance to walk to the house. A low, chill
mist was hanging in the fields. As he walked
quickly up the drive, the trees on either side
were dripping.

A man in a striped apron answered his
ring. Aucheneame did not expect visitors at
this time of the morning. Yes, Miss Dermott
was at home. What name would he say?
David stood before the fire in the morning-
parlour for what seemed a very long time.
Why was she so slow in presenting herself?
Was she afraid of him? After all, she merely
wanted to discuss things with him. He went
impatiently to the window.

How damp it was this morning! It was
becoming so foggy that he could scarcely see
the river down there in the distance across
the fields. He turned his head quickly. The
door had opened and closed. She was standing with her back to it, her hands behind her.
Her face was flushed, uncertain.

'Miss Dermott!' He moved to meet her as
she came forward hesitating. Suddenly
David's heart was caught up in a wave of
gentleness for this girl. She seemed so un-
sure, so little the imperious mistress whose
favour must be sought. He took her hand.

'I got your answer,' he said lamely.

'Yes, I–'

He looked down at her. Her eyes were brimming, though she was trying to smile. Her face was turned to him, expecting his kiss.

He kissed her and held her in his arms, letting her sob away the fullness of her heart. He could feel her body trembling against his, the body that it would be his duty to possess; its yielding contact was agreeable and vaguely stirring. All sorts of things passed through David's surprised and sharply conscious mind. He knew he was not unhappy. Life would go on now. He was holding the mother of his children in his arms. Unmated discontent was behind him. There was expectation now. There would be adjustments, but it would be easy with a gently loving woman. Their joint life would be full and prosperous. They had nothing to do but go forward.

As he stood there holding Grace Dermott, and thinking these thoughts – thoughts that at such a moment had no right to be in his mind – David made himself a solemn promise. He, and he alone, was answerable for this engagement entered into. He had offered himself as her husband, and whatever came now, he would stand by her to the end.

III

And now, this one step taken, it was easy. It was easy to sit by her and watch her happiness unfolding itself; to find her gently, shyly taking possession of him. Did David like this? She was glad, for she liked it too. Did David detest that? She was glad, for she never could bear it. She was joyfully, tenderly exploring his thoughts and his feelings.

It would have taken someone of less sensibility than David Moorhouse to remain unmoved. She loved him deeply and must have done so for some time. That was evident. There was nothing bold in her possession of him, but it was plain that her heart was fixed. He had never realised that anyone could feel so tenderly about another. It shook him to find himself the object of this tenderness. It filled him with awe. And, made as he was, it was not difficult for him to respond. It was easy to tell himself that he loved her and to tell her so in turn.

Presently her mother burst into the room. They sprang to their feet.

Mrs. Dermott's monumental person was covered by a voluminous Inverness cape. She was on the point of going out. She came to a standstill at the door with a loud 'Good gracious!'

David's eyes followed Grace as she went to her mother and told her. She hoped that her mother and father would see their way to allow it.

'I don't suppose there's any allow about it, now you've made up your minds,' Grace's mother said, advancing genially. 'What's your first name, by the way, Mr. Moorhouse? – I forget.'

'David.' Its possessor smiled. Here was normality; his familiar, everyday world.

'You had better kiss an old woman and get it over, David. I know Robert will be pleased. He's very fond of you. You had better stay to lunch, then go into Glasgow and see him at the office. It's always better to get the business side of things over and done with, and then we can get on with our plans. You'll come back for the weekend. Grace and you will want to see each other, and there will be so much for us to talk about. I'll probably spend Sunday writing letters.'

David smiled and submitted. He wondered that Grace said so little. But it was evident to him that Mrs. Dermott's daughter was used to this kind of thing. There was no mistaking the older woman's pleasure, and she was showing it in the way that came most natural to her – by going into an orgy of arranging.

Already he was being made to feel a part of the mechanism of the Dermotts' world. It was something stronger than himself. But he was rather pleased than otherwise. Its restrictions would not chafe. It would suit him very well. He must do now what he was told, and let things take their conventional course.

Sometime during next week polite Glasgow would open its morning paper to read that Mr. David Moorhouse, youngest brother of Mr. Mungo Ruanthorpe-Moorhouse of Duntrafford, Ayrshire, had engaged himself to marry Grace, only daughter of Mr. Robert Dermott of Aucheneame, Dumbartonshire, and Chairman of Dermott Ships Limited. And on the whole this would give David satisfaction. He was taking the road he wanted to go.

Chapter Nine

Lucy Rennie had her lodging in Garnethill. It may seem strange, perhaps, that a young woman of Miss Rennie's attainments should live in the quarter of Glasgow that has long been assigned to theatrical folks and to undistinguished foreigners, but she was a woman of the world and could very well look after herself. Yet there was nothing of the 'New Woman' about her. 'New Women' were pugnacious, brandished umbrellas and had big feet – or thus the comic papers of the time showed them. But for all that, Miss Rennie was fully qualified to go her own ways according to her own not uncharming fashion. She had not been a music student forced to live anyhow in London and Paris without learning independence. She knew very well when the polite conventions could be useful. But she had no scruples over breaking them when they were merely a drag. The rooms she occupied were better than most of their kind. They had been recommended to her by a fellow-singer, and they suited her purpose. They were clean, had an air of gentility, and were not threadbare. There was a piano that was usable, and her landlady, a former actress, was a motherly soul who did not bother her with questions.

As she sat by her fire, plump and pink in a warm dressing-gown, drinking a final cup of breakfast tea, and looking very much like the heroine of the novel a French acquaintance had lent her, two letters were brought. The first was in her father's hand – a laborious farmer's hand, one that seldom held a pen. It was a letter in reply to one of her own, and it contained a reproach that although she had been in Scotland for some time now, she had not yet bothered to see her family in Ayrshire. Her father reminded her that bygones were bygones; that her independence would not be criticised, and that those at home were anxious to see her.

She folded the letter thoughtfully. She had promised herself to go at New Year, but that was still some weeks away. She would visit the old man before that. It was only fair, perhaps. She had paid a flying visit when her mother died some three years ago. Since then she had not seen him. It would be more of a duty than a pleasure. The past nine years lay between her and the people at home. She had struggled, and studied, and lived this way and that. Now she had work of her own, behaviour of her own, tastes of her own. She did not intend to change them. Her mind went back to the man who had paid for her first lessons in London. She had been wise to free herself of him quickly, to go on by herself. That episode had been unpleasant, but it had taught her her world.

She brushed these thoughts out of her mind, and settling down once more, she broke the seal of the other letter. It was from Mrs. Arthur Moorhouse. The letter was conventionally kind. She had discussed the matter with her husband and, like Mrs. Moorhouse herself, he was delighted and grateful to Miss Rennie for all the trouble she was taking. They hoped to have some of official Glasgow present, through the good services of their sister, who was the wife of Baillie George McNairn. Miss Rennie would certainly remember her as Mary Moorhouse.

Lucy sat wondering now why she had bothered to offer Mrs. Arthur Moorhouse her services. Because she held it as a rule always to make a good impression when she could? Or because she had been spontaneously moved by the little, ragged children? But it was strange that she should be doing it for the wife of a Moorhouse. Her father had never liked the Moorhouse family much. She had forgotten why. Perhaps it was that they were irritatingly prosperous, working for their prosperity, and in the case of Mungo Moorhouse, the eldest, marrying into prosperity. And now only yesterday she had read in the morning paper that the youngest Moorhouse was to make an excellent match. In childhood, David had been a friend of hers. They had bird-nested and gone to the village school together. But the Moorhouses were so conventional, so cut to a pattern, such complacent, Scotch provincials.

Yet, an appearance in Mrs. Arthur Moorhouse's drawing-room would do her no harm professionally. At all events it was letting her name be known. Mrs. Moorhouse seemed a pleasant sort of woman, and one among whose friends she might later find rich pupils. Lucy got up, took pen and ink, and informed Mrs. Moorhouse that the day appointed would suit her very well. She also wrote to her father that she would be with him at Greenhead Farm the following weekend.

II

Miss Rennie was not a famous prima donna. She was a working musician who had to cut her coat according to her cloth. It was not her custom to buy a first-class ticket for a railway journey, when a third-class ticket would do. But this afternoon it had been very cold, snow was threatening, and she had made up her mind that, for all the additional expense, it would be worth her while travelling in comfort to her father's farm in central Ayrshire.

As she came through from the booking-hall she found herself under the gigantic glass arch of the new railway station of St. Enoch's. For a moment she looked about her with curiosity. It was one of the sights of Glasgow, this great station which was barely yet completed, and its novelty caught her interest.

Her train was waiting. Lucy found an empty first-class carriage, wrapped her travelling-rug about her and sat down. There was a Friday-night animation about other travellers. Weekending was coming much into vogue. Businessmen who could afford to live in the mansion houses that heretofore had been occupied by the gentry, were beginning more and more to gather their friends about them from Friday night to Monday morning, to forget for two days of the week at least that they were men of business, and to ape the ways of the people whose houses they were increasingly coming to occupy.

Presently, as she sat idly watching the crowd pass her window, hoping, as every railway traveller hopes, that she would be left in peace, her interest was aroused on seeing Mrs. Arthur Moorhouse pass down the platform accompanied by a woman who seemed in some way familiar. The two women passed her, looked in without recognition, then came back, opened the door, and the woman who accompanied Mrs. Moorhouse got in. As the train was on the point of going she laid down her belongings quickly, then turned to the open window to bid her companion goodbye.

As Mrs. Moorhouse had not seen her, Miss Rennie did not feel there was anything to be gained by making herself known. Presently the train moved off, slowly puffing its way out of the great new station into the evening, rounding the old steeple of the Merchants' House, crossing a windswept, leaden Clyde, passing the growing suburbs on the south side of the river, and speeding out into the open country.

Miss Rennie examined her travelling companion with some curiosity. Herself a farmer's daughter, she knew very well, merely from the look of her, that this was a woman of the county. There was nothing of the town about her country clothes, her stout boots, and the air with which she arranged herself and her parcels. Presently she remembered. This was Miss Ruanthorpe, the daughter of her father's landlord, old Sir Charles Ruanthorpe of Duntrafford. She had not seen Miss Ruanthorpe for some ten years. But, of course, now she was not Miss Ruanthorpe any longer. She was the wife of Mungo Moorhouse of the Laigh Farm. Sitting demurely in her corner, Miss Rennie examined her fellow-passenger with interest. So this rather distinguished woman was the new bride? They said in the county that she had pursued the farmer of the Laigh Farm for years.

The train jogged on across the wintry country. Neither of the women exchanged a word. It was evident to Lucy that Mrs. Mungo Moorhouse had no idea who she was. And a tenant's daughter could be of no great interest. The journey was tedious. The train stopped at this station and that. Doors slammed bleakly as passengers alighted on windy platforms. Interest in Mrs. Moorhouse had quickly evaporated. It was too cold to be interested in anything. There was nothing to do but sit grimly, with her eyes shut, waiting for the train to arrive.

Suddenly she became aware that Mrs. Mungo Moorhouse was asking something of her. The request was a strange one on such an evening. She asked if she might let some air in, as she felt the carriage strangely stuffy. Lucy opened her eyes in surprise. She saw that the colour was gone from her companion's face. In another moment Mrs. Moorhouse had fainted. This was alarming. For a moment she did not know what to do. But she was not a young woman who lost her head. She succeeded in laying Mrs. Moorhouse flat along the seat and undoing anything that might constrict her breathing. Presently Lucy saw with much relief that she was coming to herself. That was better. She remembered a little flask of spirits, that, as a person whose calling required her to travel much, she always carried with her.

Now Mrs. Moorhouse was sitting up again, tremulous a little but restored, and apologising for doing anything so silly. It had never happened to her before, she protested. She was sincerely sorry for having caused the young lady any sort of shock.

III

Mungo Moorhouse – or Mungo Ruanthorpe-Moorhouse, as he was now called in deference to the wishes of his eighty-year-old father-in-law, Sir Charles Ruanthorpe, Baronet, of Duntrafford, Ayrshire – stood in the midst of the prosperity he had married himself into, hastily swallowing down cups of tea. He had come back early from overseeing his farm, for in less than an hour he was to meet his wife Margaret at the railway station. As the winter evening had turned very cold, he had come home first to fetch an additional rug or two and a warm wrap, so that Margaret should not be chilled in the open pony-trap.

Mungo was nervous. He was forty-four and his wife was forty. They had been married for some three months. It was late to be starting life. And late for Margaret to be paying the kind of visit she had been paying to a Glasgow doctor today. But they were both country bred and strong as horses, and the hope of an heir, even if his surname had to be Ruanthorpe-Moorhouse instead of Ruanthorpe, was the one thing that old Sir Charles and Lady Ruanthorpe clung to. If Margaret's news was good tonight it would give the old people a new lease of life. He put down his empty cup and, going to the window, pushed back the heavy curtains, trying to look out. In the darkness it was difficult to see anything but the lamps of the trap moving up and down in front of the house, as a groom walked the pony back and forth to keep it warm. Presently he saw that a light powdering of snow was lying on the sill of the window. This was annoying. He turned back into the warm little Dower House parlour. He would have to go at once, to give himself time. The road might be difficult. It would be dangerous to hurry.

The fire was burning well enough, but he lifted the coal-scuttle in his strong farmer's hands and emptied additional coal upon it. Margaret must be warm. She had spent last night at his brother Arthur's house in Glasgow. It was the first night since their marriage that they had been apart. He was as eager as a youngster over his wife's home-coming.

As he struggled into his heavy driving-coat in the little hall, he shouted in the hope that some servant would hear him: 'Ye better keep an eye on that fire.'

A maid came running, a surprised look on her face. 'Is anything wrong, sir?'

'There's a lot of coal on that fire. Watch it doesna fall out.'

'Yes, sir.'

He was not yet in the way of ringing bells and giving orders to starched parlourmaids. He had shouted to the girls at the Laigh Farm when he wanted them. That had been good enough. He was not like his brother David, who had been caught young and turned into a gentleman. But Margaret seemed to like his farmer's ways, so why should he bother?

On the doorstep he stood looking about him into the darkness. Feathers of snow were wheeling slowly down around him. He shouted to the groom, 'Are ye there, Davie?'

The man brought the trap over.

'It's a pity to see that snow,' Mungo said.

'Aye. It'll be a cold run home for the mistress.'

'I'll need to watch where I'm going.' Mungo ran his hand down the neck of his pony, then he climbed in and took the reins. For an instant the groom stood watching the beams from the lamp of the trap as they lit up the snow on either side of the short Dower House drive. Presently there was nothing but the sound of hoof-claps lightly muffled by the new-fallen snow. The man took a short cut through the shrubbery to the Duntrafford stables and the harness-room fire.

IV

The snow was falling thickly as Mungo, having covered his pony as best he could, waited in front of the country railway station. This delay was tedious. It was no night for a beast to be kept standing.

But as Mungo stood at his pony's head, the snow alighting gently upon his shoulders, he was strangely excited. What news was Margaret bringing him? It seemed quite unreal that, at his age, things should have taken this turn. He had gone on for so long working; first, for his father at the Laigh Farm, and then later by himself. He had taken his life for granted. He had been interested and busy. That had been enough. He had no opportunity to marry in his younger days, and had not, perhaps, even thought of doing so. Then, as it seemed to him suddenly, he was the husband of the laird's daughter. And this very night he was standing in the snow, his placid heart beating like the heart of a twenty-year-old, waiting to hear from her if he was to be the father of the laird's grandchild.

Suddenly the night was pierced by the scream of a whistle. There was an increasing roar, and a splash of fiery red in the snowy darkness. The drivers of dog-carts and carriages jumped to their places. There was a rush and hurrying on the ill-lit platform. There was the beat of slowing wheels; the lighted rows of moving windows. The evening train had come to a halt.

Still holding his pony's head, Mungo stood peering anxiously through the lighted arch of the railway station. People for the village came first, chattering with friends who had come to meet them, looking up unhappily at the falling snow, wrapping themselves closer, then hurrying off on foot. Someone came out, hired the village cab, and drove off. Familiar people, businessmen and gentry, hurried into their carriages and went off to

110

their country houses. Mungo was becoming impatient. It was time his wife appeared. All the conveyances were moving or preparing to move. All except the Greenhead dog-cart. It was waiting, too, with old Tom Rennie perched up impatiently in the driving-seat.

At last Mungo saw the outline of his wife against the light of the station entrance. She was talking with a smaller woman, who seemed to be carrying her things for her. A moment later Margaret had seen him. Both women were coming across.

'Oh, there you are, Mungo. What a terrible night!' Margaret said, coming up. 'This is Miss Rennie of Greenhead, who is being very nice to me.' Mungo remembered Lucy Rennie and nodded.

'Are you all right, Mrs. Moorhouse?' Lucy was packing Margaret and her parcels into the trap.

'Quite. Now run away. There's your father waiting for you. And it's a promise that you'll come across and see me when you are here at New Year? Good. Now run. This snow is awful.'

This was no moment for ceremony. A second later the Ruanthorpe-Moorhouses, muffled to their ears, were making their cautious way home.

The road led steeply downhill. They were both of them too much of the country to engage in talk while the driver had the very

111

slippery foothold of his pony to see to. The snow had made the road uncertain, and Mungo, however much he might want to hear her news, must give his mind to the pony and the darkness. But soon they were at the foot of the hill and on the level. The little animal was trotting cautiously on familiar ground.

Margaret broke silence. 'I did a silly thing, Mungo. I suddenly fainted right away in the train. The Rennie girl from Greenhead was with me in the carriage. She gave me some brandy.'

'Are ye all right now?' Mungo was crouched over the reins; his intent eyes were trying to pierce the gloom beyond his pony's ears.

'Yes.'

He drove steadily for a moment. He was waiting for his wife to speak again, but she did not. He was driven to speak himself. 'Was that – a good sign?'

'Yes, Mungo. It was a good sign.'

'Fine.' Mungo did not belong to a breed that carries emotion on its sleeve. There was nothing he could do to show his pleasure, here in the snowy darkness. He had no command of words. But a glow was lit within him. He found himself holding the reins in his hands with greater care, straining to use his countryman's knowledge yet more skilfully. He must give his whole mind now to getting his wife home safely.

V

'Charles, what's the matter with you?' Old Lady Ruanthorpe looked down the table of the dining-room at Duntrafford. Even when they were alone, this dogged old couple persisted in dining formally.

Sir Charles, a stringy old man with mutton-chop whiskers, a black stock and velvet dinner-jacket, glared back at his wife. 'What do you mean, "matter", Meg? I'm all right.'

'You've eaten practically no dinner.'

'Surely I can eat as much as I choose to. Remember I am eighty. It's wrong for old people to eat too much.'

There was something that might have been anxiety in her determined, weather-beaten face. Lady Ruanthorpe peered at her husband over the expanse of white linen, cut-glass, hothouse fern and silver. 'Fiddle-sticks,' was all she said. Her eyes weren't too good, and the lights from the candles dazzled them a bit. But Charles had been refusing this dish and that. It was ridiculous.

A man-servant had set the fruit on the table, put the port in front of his master, and was preparing to withdraw.

'Campbell.' The old man's sharp voice brought him back.

113

'Yes, Sir Charles?'

'Look through the curtains and tell me what sort of night it is.' Sir Charles poured himself out a glass, got up and, laying one hand on the white mantelpiece for support, sipped his port and warmed himself at the fire.

The man reappeared from the window recess, through the heavy crimson velvet curtains. 'It's deep snow, Sir Charles,' he said.

'Go downstairs and ask if there's no word from the Dower House, and come back and tell me at once.'

As the servant went, Lady Ruanthorpe turned to look at her husband. 'What do you think you're up to?'

'I want to know if Margaret's back.'

'Margaret's been in Glasgow before and got back safely. She's quite fit to look after herself.'

Sir Charles grunted. 'How do you know?'

His lady went into a peal of cracked laughter. 'You're an old rascal; that's what you are.'

Sir Charles did not reply. He merely stood his port on the mantelpiece and warmed both his hands, waiting.

In a moment the man came back.

'Well, Campbell?'

'No, Sir Charles. No message.'

'Damn it! They might at least—'

'Charles, what's the matter with you? It's a

horrid snowy night. You can't expect–'

But Sir Charles was fidgeting with impatience. 'Has the snow stopped falling, Campbell?'

'Yes, Sir Charles.'

'There should be a moon. Was there one?'

'Well, it's not Campbell's fault if there wasn't.'

'Don't be frivolous, Meg.'

'There was a moon, Sir Charles.'

'Very well, then. Go and tell them to bring round the closed carriage.'

'Charles! You can't bring Margaret across here after a long day and a cold journey!'

'I have no intention. Do as I tell you, Campbell.'

The man went.

Lady Ruanthorpe was really alarmed now. She got up and crossed to her husband. 'Charles, what do you intend to do?'

'I intend to go to the Dower House, and ask Margaret if she is going to have a child.'

'I wondered.' She regarded her husband. He was looking like a stubborn child himself now. She must do what she could with him. She put a hand on his arm. 'You know you haven't been out at night for weeks now. Remember that we had Margaret's wedding in this house because you weren't well enough to go to church.'

'I tell you I'm going, Meg.' She wasn't to be allowed to put him off. Ruanthorpes had always prided themselves in doing what they wanted.

She shook his arm affectionately. 'I'm terrified for you, my dear. I'll go across quickly when the carriage comes, then come back at once and tell you.'

He did not answer, but she could feel his arm trembling. She raised her eyes to his face.

'Good gracious me, Charles! Whatever–?'

'I wouldn't have been making such a fuss if Charlie had been living.'

Their boy who had been killed in the hunting-field years ago. An old wound that had never healed. She knew now what this meant to him, or he would never have hurt her with this reminder. She summoned the years of bleak self-discipline to steady her.

'All right, Charles. There's no more to be said. We'll get you wrapped up and I'll come with you.'

VI

And so it came about that Mungo had a visit that evening from the most unexpected of guests. This stolid Ayrshire farmer took his parents-in-law on the whole calmly. They had sought him and, by his manner towards them, he never quite allowed them to forget it. Their abrupt patrician ways, so

116

different from the ways of his prim and urban relatives, worried him, usually, not at all. But tonight even he had to admit that their behaviour was unexpected. His wife and he were sitting snugly in the Dower House parlour when the door was thrown open and a bundle of clothes with Sir Charles Ruanthorpe's head at the top of it pushed itself into the room, followed by Margaret's mother. They sprang to their feet. Margaret went to him.

'Good gracious, Father! Whatever are you doing here?'

'Are you going to have a baby, Margaret?'

'You needn't shout so loud, Father. The servants will know soon enough.'

'Then you are?'

'Yes. If all goes well.'

'You had better kiss me.'

Smiling a little sheepishly, Mungo watched his wife embrace her parents. They appeared to him to have forgotten about him, or, indeed, that he had anything to do with it. For a moment he was the farmer of the Laigh Farm again, and here was the laird and his family. They were fond of making a fuss with themselves, the gentry.

'If it's a boy, his name's to be Charles,' the old man was saying.

Margaret turned to her husband. She knew there had been a good, peasant line of Mungo Moorhouses.

'What do ye think, my dear?' Mungo asked her.

'Charles has always been the name of the first boy in our family,' her father insisted.

Margaret touched her husband's arm. 'Charlie was the name of my brother, Mungo.'

'Very well, my dear, if yer baby's a boy we'll call him for yer brother Charlie.'

Mungo Moorhouse had given Sir Charles Ruanthorpe of Duntrafford his permission.

Chapter Ten

At St. Enoch's Station, Bel said goodbye to her sister-in-law Margaret with the most affectionate smile she could muster, then trudged wearily down the platform feeling she hated everybody, particularly everybody who was called, or likely to be called, Moorhouse. Yesterday, Margaret Ruanthorpe-Moorhouse had descended upon her suddenly. Then, claiming the intimacy of a married relative, she had asked Bel to accompany her upon her visit to the doctor. Bel wished Phœbe could have gone with Margaret. Phœbe knew more of the Ruanthorpes. She had often been to Duntrafford from the Laigh Farm. But the errand to the

118

specialist was a particular one. A young, unmarried girl couldn't be expected to understand Margaret's hopes and fears. So Bel had had to go with Margaret, and duly express her genteel and knowing pleasure at the coming happy but unmentionable event.

Today was Friday of the first week in December. That meant Christmas looming, with all the fuss of presents and entertainment. Tomorrow she had promised to drag herself down to the warehouse to see that poor Highland woman whose husband had lost his foot. On Tuesday of next week she had invited David's newly affianced bride and her mother to tea at Grosvenor Terrace to be introduced to David's sisters. That meant sweeping and garnishing the house on Monday. No. She had too much to worry her.

She stood at the entrance of the station for a moment grimly wondering how best she could get home. A sudden gust of icy wind made her shiver and draw her furs about her. All at once a thought came to her. She would indulge herself a little. She would call a cab and visit her mother in Monteith Row. From there she could easily get a message to her husband telling him to fetch her later. Tea and a little maternal petting was what she was needing.

The cab was chill and musty and smelt inside of leather, sawdust and horse, but Bel didn't mind. She closed her eyes and thrust her hands deeper into her muff. It was a relief merely to be sitting still. They jolted down the ramp leading from St. Enoch's Station into Argyle Street. Already, gas-flares were lighted in most of the shops. Christmas decorations were appearing everywhere. Windows were brighter and more tempting than ever. There was tinsel and coloured paper everywhere. The very badness of the times seemed to be forcing the shops to make their wares appear more desirable.

As the cab threaded its way through the traffic, Bel, in spite of her weariness, could not help craning forward to see what it was they were exhibiting in this window and that. Presently she was paying off the cab in front of the entrance to her mother's flat in Monteith Row.

Mrs. Barrowfield, who had been feeling dull, was delighted to see Bel. It had been cold this morning, and Maggie her elderly housemaid had, on being commanded to deliver an opinion, duly delivered the opinion expected of her, and advised the old lady to stay in. This may have been safe advice, but a day at home was not entertaining. Mrs. Barrowfield therefore received her daughter with great energy and affection, and sat her down on the other side of the fire.

Almost at once Bel began to be sorry she had come. Her mother, having finished her own tea, was sitting bolt upright in front of her preparing to fire off reproofs, questions and advice.

'Well, my dear, where have ye been? Ye look as if ye have been running yerself off yer feet.'

'So I have, Mother, but I can't help it.'

'Well, you *should* help it. Nobody'll thank you for doing it. Where were ye today?'

Bel had to go through the entire story of Mrs. Mungo's visit and the probability of her having a baby. The old lady didn't take this news particularly well. She had hoped that the Ruanthorpe-Moorhouses would remain childless. Her daughter's children might then in time have become, in some part, their legatees.

'And what's all this about David?'

That had to be gone through, too. Then Bel had to listen carefully to the story of the rise of Robert Dermott's fortunes. A story that was common knowledge in Glasgow, and had already been recounted to her many times – usually, as now, with the purpose of impressing upon her that her husband's brother was marrying no one of any real consequence after all.

'Grace Dermott and her mother are coming to tea on Tuesday. That means polishing and cleaning the house.'

'Ye'll kill yerself,' Mrs. Barrowfield said with every evidence of satisfaction. 'And you'll only have yerself to thank.'

'I won't be able to thank myself, if I'm dead,' Bel smiled bleakly.

But Mrs. Barrowfield only fixed her through her steel spectacles and said, 'Find out what David wants me to give him for a wedding-present. He's a friend o' mine, is David.' Like many old ladies, she was pleased to imagine she had a special understanding of young men.

Bel sighed. She had come hoping to find the old lady sympathetic. She had wanted to confide in her about the Rennie concert, and about her worries over the slum people that Arthur was proposing to put into the coach-house. But it was no use today. She would merely be scolded for everything. Such was her mother's mood.

Presently Mrs. Barrowfield rose and fetched a pencil and paper. 'And just when I have ye, my dear, I want ye to tell me what I'm to get for all the bairns' Christmas presents. Let me see, there's your three, and Mary McNairn's four, and Sophia's two. Then I aye give Phœbe something, and there's you and Arthur. I'll not bother with David this year, seeing he's getting a good wedding-present. But there's the minister and the usual folk in the church.'

Bel put up a beaten protest. How could her mother feel so well and strong? 'Oh, not this evening, Mother! I can't think. I've had a busy day.'

'Get away with ye! It'll not take a minute.' She got down in front of Bel and began writing, her hard grey curls dangling on either side of her energetic head.

It was no good. Bel had to go through the list, and there were several more that occurred to her mother as she went along. Each had to be considered and argued about, and she had to suffer not a little exhausting contradiction.

Arthur's arrival was as a straw to a drowning woman. Mrs. Barrowfield greeted her son-in-law in high good-humour, pressed a glass of wine upon him, and tried to make them stay for a meal. But by hidden signs Bel indicated to her husband that at all costs they must go.

So Arthur, like a dutiful husband, much regretted. Everybody would be anxious about them at home. It was a pity, he said waggishly, that they all hadn't these strange American things called Bell telephones that some of the more progressive doctors were said to be getting in this winter, so that they could consult each other in dire emergency without leaving their own houses. But until such a time it was kinder to arrive home when you were expected, or people would jump to the conclusion that you were under the hoofs of a tramway horse.

Mrs. Barrowfield said she didn't believe a

123

word about these distant speaking things, and what would people be up to next? She embraced Bel with energy, thanked her almost pathetically for her visit, and told her to remember that her mother was a worn-out, lonely old woman, who was always grateful when she could spare the time to come and see her.

Well aware that all this last was for Arthur's benefit, Bel kissed her mother affectionately enough, and went off on her husband's arm. She turned to him at the end of the Row. 'Would it be terribly extravagant to take a cab home, Arthur?'

'It's a long way. Do ye feel ye need it, my dear?'

'I do.' How comforting of him not to ask any more questions! She wouldn't tell him she had wasted money on one today already.

Once settled in the cab, Bel affectionately propped herself against her husband's shoulder and sentimentally held his hand. The regular trotting of the horse made her sleepy. For the first time today she was contented and happy. There was something soothing about Arthur. He wasn't really a bad old thing. Perhaps, after all, she concluded to herself dreamily, Moorhouses did have their uses.

II

On the following morning Bel had all the symptoms of a bad cold. There was nothing for it but bed. This was a nuisance. She had the arrangements for the weekend to see to. And, in addition, she had promised to go down town to see the Highland woman and to arrange, if the woman looked civilised enough, for her charitable sojourn in the coachman's quarters in Grosvenor Terrace Lane. Now Arthur said she would have to allow Phœbe to go in her stead.

Bel was not sure about this. Phœbe was so impulsive. She had no balance when it came to lame ducks. The sight of one was quite enough to rob her of all common sense. There was always some rescued mongrel or kitten in the empty stable at the back being fed and tended by Phœbe. Much to the delight of Bel's own children, of course. But it was all very well. Phœbe did not stop to remember that such animals might carry disease.

Why couldn't he pay the woman her man's wages and let her remain where she was for another week? she demanded huskily of Arthur as he brushed his hair. After the evasive fashion of husbands, Arthur replied that he had better see. See what? Bel demanded. But by this time Arthur was on his way downstairs to breakfast. And when

Sarah, Bel's housemaid, brought up her breakfast tray, she told her that Miss Phœbe had gone out with the master. That was that. There was nothing now for Bel to do but feel sorry for herself.

Later in the morning Phœbe came back from the meeting important and excited. She had found lame ducks after her own heart. The woman, she told Bel, was a poor, proud creature, and the two little children were sickly mites. She had arranged for them to come this afternoon. One of Arthur's warehouse men was fetching them and their belongings in a cart.

Bel heaved a worried sigh. If she had arranged this herself, she would, of course, have been uplifted by her own kindness. But as Arthur and his sister had arranged it, she was filled with disapproval. The roses of her bedroom wallpaper danced unsteadily before her eyes. She felt feverish forebodings. These urchins would probably infect her own children with every known disease.

'I'm worried about this, Phœbe,' she said. 'Did the children look clean?'

'How could they be clean?' Phœbe demanded of her with sudden and surprising passion. 'I know what these slum rooms look like. Are you forgetting that once I brought Arthur out of one of them?'

Bel never forgot that. However puzzling, however maddening this girl might be, Bel was never to forget a night four years ago when her world had stood still with horror because her three-year-old son had been kidnapped. She would never forget the ragged, filthy girl of fourteen who had appeared out of the cruel darkness dragging the child to safety. That was a link between Bel and Phœbe that would never be broken. Passionate self-will could have another name even in a difficult half-grown girl. The name was courage.

This was the first time, indeed, that Phœbe had referred to it, and Bel guessed rightly that this slum woman and her children had reawakened echoes in Phœbe's stormy heart.

'What a dirty wee brat you looked!' Bel replied with intentional triviality. After all there was no purpose in allowing Phœbe to excite herself with memories.

The handsome, flushed child, standing at the foot of her bed, did not reply to this. Her colour merely deepened for an instant, and a flicker of contempt showed in her face. 'Anyway, Henry can help me with them when he comes this afternoon.' She turned and went to join the family at their midday meal.

Bel smiled to herself in spite of a swollen nose and pricking eyes. It seemed a strange sort of love-making that went on between this eager and restless couple. Either they were quarrelling or engrossing themselves in some quite unlikely occupation. And helping a slum woman with her flitting was one of the most unlikely.

III

David had not been looking forward to Tuesday. This perhaps was not unnatural. At almost no time does a young man see his own family in a more critical light than at the moment when he must present them to his future wife. At no time do relatives seem more homely and inadequate. No. Tuesday was merely an ordeal to be got through.

Grace and her mother drove into the City in the morning. David was asked to join them at their midday meal. He found Robert Dermott with them. The Dermotts were, each of them, warm-hearted people in their way, and their pleasure in David's company was not assumed. Placed between Robert Dermott and his wife, David was compelled to listen to an account of the appalling state of British merchant shipping on one side, and on the other, to hear, minutely and at length, just what Mrs. Dermott's plans for Christmas were, and how very greatly they must now be altered as a result of his engagement to her daughter. David did everything he could to sustain both conversations at once, which was not difficult, as his future parents-in-law were doing all the talking.

When the meal was over he rose to go. He would meet the ladies later and all three would drive out in the carriage to Bel's house in Grosvenor Terrace. Robert Dermott came with him.

Once out in the street, the old man caught his arm. 'Ye haven't a minute to come up to the office, David?'

David thought he could find that minute.

'Come away, then.' Mr. Dermott said no more, but turned in the direction of the office of Dermott Ships Limited. In some moments they were there, and David was following on the heels of the chairman of the company through the great main doorway. He felt self-conscious as he passed through the large outer office filled with clerks, who, at the sight of the old man, had suddenly been seized with an intense interest in their work. They passed through a smaller office with some three or four senior clerks in it. Among them was David's friend Stephen Hayburn. As he was hurried on, David allowed himself a hasty smirk of recognition, and Stephen shut one eye.

The chairman's private room was like every other chairman's private room in Glasgow. It had a great mahogany desk, a deep, Turkey carpet, an extravagantly blazing fire and composite photographs of various bodies of important gentlemen of the City hanging in faded gold frames against

Pompeiian red walls.

'Sit down, boy.' David found himself affectionately thrust into a worn leather chair out of which the padding was bursting. For a time the old man fanned out his coat-tails in front of the fire and looked down at him, saying nothing. David waited.

'I want my son-in-law to come into this business,' Robert Dermott fired at him suddenly; then, as many businessmen will, he stood watching the effect of his words.

David's colour changed. 'It's very kind, Mr. Dermott,' he said lamely.

'Kind? Everything I have in the world will go to you and your wife someday. I want ye to learn to look after it. Dermott Ships Limited is not all mine. But most of it is. And I don't want ye to throw it away.'

David stood up. The Dermotts' love and generosity were closing round him in a way that was frightening. The idea of joining Dermott Ships alarmed him. The family did not consider him a good businessman, and he knew they were right. As a boy in his teens, Arthur had taken him, drilled him, and set his somewhat frivolous feet in the ways that a sound businessman's feet should take. The snob within him told him that he would rather be in ships than in cheese. But that was only one side of it. The proposition overwhelmed him.

'I would like to talk to my brother Arthur

about this,' he said at length. 'You see, I owe everything to him, Mr. Dermott.'

'I'm glad to hear you say it, David. Ye're a good boy. But yer brother would be mad to refuse ye a chance like this.' He put his great hand on David's shoulder. 'I'll come across with ye and see yer brother, if ye like.'

'I'll speak to him myself first, Mr. Dermott.'

'Very well.'

'And thank you again.' David held out his hand, feeling like a boy who had been to tea with the headmaster.

'Get away with ye. Ye belong to us now, laddie.' He struck the young man's shoulder a resounding blow of affection. David was amazed at the warmth of this great, over-emotional Highlander. He was glad to get himself out of the room, to find himself alone in the street.

IV

Bel was forever setting her stage and hoping that everything would run according to her programme. The facts of this afternoon's arrangements were these. She had asked Mrs. Robert Dermott of Aucheneame to tea, together with her daughter, Grace. And she had asked David's sisters to come and meet them.

Out of this, Bel had painted for herself a picture. On Tuesday afternoon she would be found by her chief visitors, calm and poised and, she hoped, not entirely without good looks, sitting in a flower-filled drawing-room, graciously ready to take her newest sister-in-law to her elegant bosom. They would have a charming talk, with just the proper amount of emotion in it, then she would give them tea from a table spread with delicate lace and covered with glittering silver and fine china. Later, David's elder sisters would appear, drink tea, and be presented. And through all this she herself would move, smiling and holding the social reins. Encouraging here – restraining there. And, though she did not quite admit it, the hope was hidden somewhere within her, that David's future relatives would in due course take their leave feeling that it would be a privilege to be allied to anyone so charming and so accomplished as Mrs. Arthur Moorhouse.

That was the picture as Bel saw it. By Tuesday morning she knew that some of the details at least must be imperfect. For one thing, she herself would not be in her best looks. Her cold was receding, but her nose was still red. And when she had got up yesterday, she had felt weak on her legs and unfit to see to such important things as dusting, sweeping and the buying and arranging of flowers. Phœbe had said she would see to everything, but that wasn't quite the same. She was much too impetuous, and prepared to think that anything would do.

Then, while she was scarcely yet ready to receive her guests, Sophia and Mary arrived. Bel was annoyed. She had asked them to come later, hoping to have the Dermotts to herself at first. Now she had only to enter her drawing-room to feel that indefinable closing of the family ranks.

'Bel, dear, what a dreadful cold you have!' Mary said. 'Is it wise to be having a tea-party today? As I was just saying to Sophia and Phœbe, I think it's wonderful how you keep yourself on the go.'

Sophia, who had been chattering to Phœbe, turned the flood on Bel. 'I hope you don't mind us coming a little soon, dear. But you see we've heard so little about all this. It's been so secret. But, then, these things have to be secret till the last minute, don't they? It wouldn't really be suitable if they weren't, would it? But, as I said to William just last night, "Trust Bel. She'll know all about this!"'

Bel had no intention of telling David's sisters anything of his confidences to herself. As she sat looking at Sophia, she noted with some satisfaction that she had left her muff to dry too near the fire, as some of its hair was singed, and it had lost its lustre. 'It's all been a great surprise, hasn't it?' was all she said.

'And Phœbe tells me that Margaret Ruan-thorpe is going to have a baby,' Mary said with a conventional show of pleasure.

Bel winced a little. Young girls like Phœbe shouldn't be talking about such things. Even to their own married sisters. That was what came of being a farmer's daughter, she supposed.

But Mary had thrown a stone that was bound to cause ripples.

'Of course, we think it isn't wise,' Sophia said. 'After all, Margaret must be forty. Well – I mean forty is not quite the age to be having a first baby.'

Bel took the precaution of sending Phœbe downstairs to see after something quite unnecessary, then the three married ladies got their heads together. She had much to tell of Margaret's visit. What the doctor had said. In what respect she must be careful. How she had taken the news. Bel couldn't help enjoying the telling. Nor could she think so ill of Sophia and Mary as she had done a moment ago. After all, they were comfortable, familiar creatures to gossip with. They had forgotten she had a cold, and were exposing themselves to it freely in their eagerness to catch every detail of this important family news, as it fell from Bel's still-swollen lips. And so Bel, Mary and Sophia had quite forgotten appearances, and were deep in talk, when Mrs. Dermott,

Miss Dermott and Mr. David were announced. Hurriedly Bel rose to receive them, feeling all too acutely that her reception of them lacked the poise and graciousness she had planned.

David did not enjoy this women's tea-party. As was natural, he was very conscious of everything his relatives did. He had counted on Bel to maintain an atmosphere of refined distinction. But she had, it seemed, a bad cold, and appeared ridiculously fussed as she poured out tea.

Mrs. Dermott's habit of talking loudly made, for those who did not know her, the easy interchange of polite and suitable ideas a difficult matter. Grace, instead of behaving as the honoured guest, was apologetically handing round bread and butter. And as for the others, David decided it was no use expecting the family to be anything else than the family. At last, however, they settled themselves down in some sort of way. Grace and Phœbe beside Bel at the tea-table, and Mary and Sophia with Mrs. Dermott.

As he moved about he saw that Grace's eyes were upon him. It was strange how little confidence she had in herself, how often her look was asking for his approval. She was a gentle creature. He was fond of her.

He wandered for a moment to the window and looked out. The offer he had received from Robert Dermott worried him. What was he to say to Arthur? His brother had done everything for him. He felt that if Arthur wanted him to stay in the business in the Candleriggs, he was bound to do so. Yet he could not deny that it would be great advancement to be one of the firm of Dermott Ships. And he knew that it would please Grace.

David stood uneasily gazing through the bare December trees out into Great Western Road. An almost empty tramcar, its mud-bespattered horses trotting dispiritedly, was making its way to the Kirklee terminus. A couple of hansoms, their wheels casting a spray of snowy slush, were flying downhill into town.

Over there across the road in the white Botanic Gardens there was no sign of life. The gas-jets in the street lamps shone pale in the fading daylight.

Yes. It was all bound up with Grace. Everything was bound up with Grace now. He could never escape that. He was never free now from an unnamed feeling, an unnamed compulsion. He must keep compensating – making up for something he was unable to give her. He had not defined this even to himself. But it was there, influencing all his plans.

'I've been sent to tell you to come and talk to us.' He felt a hand in his own, and turned to find Grace beside him. He came back

136

with her, recalled to his duty. He was pleased to see that Grace had made friends with Bel, and that even Phœbe, who could on occasion be so withdrawn that there was no understanding her, had unbent, and was telling her of some slum family that had become her latest hobby.

Sophia and Mrs. Dermott in their group were happily talking simultaneously.

'And you see, Mrs. Dermott, in a family like mine,' Sophia was saying, 'it's very difficult to have meals at regular times. You see, my husband never will tell me when he's coming home, so he just has to be fed when he appears. And the children are worse. I was just saying to the servant this morning–'

And through all this Mrs. Dermott was explaining: 'So I had to tell these women that if they were taking that attitude there was nothing more to be said. Of course admittedly it was annoying for me. I had given a lot of my time and money, and the gardener had sent several bunches of greenhouse flowers to decorate the platform first, and be sold to help the funds afterwards. But then it was silly of me to expect–'

Mary was sitting between them pretending to give this rather disjointed conversation some kind of cohesion, but in reality she was making the most of a particularly delicious chocolate cake that was one of the specialities of Bel's kitchen, the recipe for which Bel was

– Mary suspected by intention – always forgetting to give her.

This was not the kind of meeting David had foreseen, but they all seemed to approve of each other, and everyone seemed happy. He went back to the party at the tea-table.

'I've just been telling Bel,' Grace said, looking up at him, and blushing to find herself using Mrs. Arthur Moorhouse's first name, 'that I don't think she should have this charity concert she's telling me about until after Christmas. She's got a terrible cold, David, and, as she says herself, she's got all her Christmas things to see to.' She appealed to Phœbe. Phœbe, who had never really troubled to think about it, was quite prepared to agree.

'But Miss Rennie will have left Glasgow after Christmas,' Bel protested.

'Perhaps not immediately after. Write and ask her at once. David, couldn't you take Miss Rennie a letter this evening, after we go?'

'Yes, of course.'

Bel allowed herself to be persuaded. It was nice of Grace to show this thoughtfulness. Grace, she felt, was going to be on her side of the family camp.

The carriage was announced. Mrs. Dermott rose to go. She held out her hand to Sophia, but Sophia did not take it.

'No, my dear, I'm coming down to see you

off at the door. We'll all go!'

Bel was amazed at the state of easy familiarity between her least presentable sister-in-law and the forbidding Mrs. Robert Dermott. Sophia's suggestion seemed to have pleased her. Etiquette was being flaunted at every turn. They all trooped downstairs and waved the carriage off. Everything was friendship and goodwill. Sophia even offered Mrs. Dermott her singed muff as additional comfort against the coldness of the journey.

Chapter Eleven

It was quite dark when David left Grosvenor Terrace bearing Bel's letter to Miss Rennie. His sisters had waited just long enough to express their approval of his choice – an approval that was not altogether conventional; for Grace Dermott had been anxious to please.

Bel's note was short. It was better, she had determined, for David to try to see Miss Rennie himself and explain to her how things really stood. Bel knew that she could depend upon David's tact. If Miss Rennie were not in, he had promised Bel to go back at a time when he should find her.

It was damp and cold as David stood, huddled in his greatcoat, waiting for a tramcar to come down from the turning place at Kirklee. He felt dispirited. After years of bachelor freedom, of few obligations, of easy friendships, responsibility was gathering itself around him.

At last a car was approaching. He signed to it to stop. He settled himself gratefully, as the horses resumed their measured trot. It had been, after all, a day of strain. And tomorrow he must speak to Arthur about Robert Dermott's wish to have him in Dermott Ships.

At Hill Street he got down and began making his way up into Garnethill. The street was not well lit. He had to peer about in the darkness, seeking the number. Once, thinking he had come up too far, he asked his way of a young woman standing beneath a street lamp. She directed him eagerly, offering, indeed, to come with him. He noted her 'English' voice and her too ready laughter, as he protested that he could find his destination very well by himself.

Miss Rennie's landlady assured him that her young lady was at home, and that, although Miss Rennie had just come back from the country, she was sure she would see him. He stood in the dim little hall, lit by a single gas-jet, which for economy's sake had been turned down to a peep, while the woman opened the door, went inside and shut it behind her. David was kept waiting for just such time as it takes a self-conscious young woman who has thrown aside her outdoor things to make herself hastily tidy.

II

'David Moorhouse!' Lucy Rennie came forward and gave him both her hands. The landlady closed the door behind them. 'I would have known you anywhere, David,' she said, bringing him to a seat by a cheerful fire. 'Would you have known me?'

'Of course, Lucy.' David was surprised at himself. In the stress of events it had not somehow occurred to him that he was coming to meet an old friend. She was not much changed after fifteen years. Her face was still round and gay, and her eyes still danced with mischief. Maturity, womanliness and a pleasant, cultivated voice were added. That was all.

They sat, as people in a like situation will, gazing at each other with frank, unaffected curiosity, their thoughts going back to such things as hunting for peewit's eggs in the high Ayrshire furrows, or standing hand in hand, two frightened little children, as the 'otter hunt' – pink coats, baying hounds and yapping terriers – made their alarming way past them as they played by the river.

141

'You're a very grand young man now, David!'

'You're a very grand young woman, Lucy.'

Lucy laughed. 'No; not very grand, David. I've got to work for my living. I've learnt my way about. That's all.'

David brought out Bel's letter. While Lucy broke the seal and read it, he sat looking about him. The little sitting-room was warm and comfortable. In addition to its cheerful plush-covered furniture, it was made gay with innumerable knick-knacks, a painted tambourine, feathery pampas grasses dyed in bright colours, painted fans, silk bows on velvet picture-frames; the random decorations of some unselective, feminine mind. There was a silk-fronted piano piled with music. Supper was laid. Lucy must just have come in. Furs and other outdoor things topped by a smart little hat and veil were lying on a chair to one side.

His eyes turned to re-examine the girl who was living thus independently. It was unthinkable that his sister Phœbe should live unchaperoned like this. And yet what was there that was wrong about it? Why should it be unusual for a man to be sitting here, the one visitor in the rooms of a young woman who was, after all, a childhood's friend?

The vague feeling that in some way he was overstepping propriety, amused and stirred this very conventional young man with new and not unpleasant sensations. Somehow it touched his manhood. Lucy Rennie, he felt, was putting full dependence on his chivalry. The situation was novel. As she bent over Bel's note, she looked different from the women he was accustomed to. She was plump, and her dark hair was piled up on her head like a Frenchwoman's. As she looked up, folding the paper at the same time, the expression of her round face was quick and responsive.

'I'm sorry about Mrs. Moorhouse, David. I like her so much, you know.'

David explained about Bel. Earnestly excusing her, hoping that Lucy would understand and forgive, and in the end, daring to hope that when New Year was over, she would still be in Glasgow long enough to make it possible to give her recital of songs.

Lucy understood everything. She would be at home in Ayrshire over the New Year, but thereafter she would try to spend a day or two in Glasgow in order to fulfil her promise. She would write a note to Mrs. Arthur Moorhouse to reassure her. David thanked her and rose to go.

'David! Already? It's so nice to see you. Must you go away? There was so much I wanted to say to you.' Lucy stood up and put her hand on the bell-rope. 'Look, David, I was just going to have supper. I don't know what there is to eat, but as you've dared to penetrate into Bohemia, why don't you stay and share it with me? I wanted to tell you I had seen your brother Mungo and his wife. I'm just back from Greenhead. And I want to have a look at you just for a little longer.' Her smile had a whimsical appeal in it.

David was tempted. It was pleasant here. For the first time today, he did not feel that all the cares of the world were pressing close about him. This, after all, was an old and harmless friendship. If Lucy's manner was flattering, if she was intensely feminine – that was how she was made, and it could have no significance.

She saw his hesitation. 'David, I believe I am being too unconventional for you! Really! It wouldn't be the first time we had picnicked together, would it? But perhaps I've been a gipsy too long. Perhaps I am forgetting what's proper. I must leave it to you.'

The landlady was standing by, awaiting orders. It would be churlish, David felt, to walk out – churlish and gauche. He turned gaily to the grey-haired woman. 'Will you allow me to have supper with Miss Rennie?'

The woman was surprised at his flushed face, his refinement, his air of innocence. This young man was a gentleman; an unusual type for hereabouts. 'I think we might allow that, sir. I'll bring another cup.'

'I'm so glad, David. I'll show you where to put your coat.'

144

The meal was cosy and gay. They told each other what they had done with themselves since they had parted in their teens. David was surprised to find how much more Lucy had seen and done than he had. She spoke French fluently, she told him, having spent some time as a student-governess in Paris. She had sung in many famous London houses. Although she had been only a paid musician, she had been in some kind of contact with many celebrated people, and had used her eyes and her ears. She was able to give him many amusing impressions of them. It was a world beyond the provincial climbings of David Moorhouse.

Presently they talked of the old days, when the little boy from the Laigh Farm had waited at the end of the road for the little girl from Greenhead, and together they had trudged the mile or so to the village school. There had been no great friendship between the families, but the children gave each other companionship and a sense of protection in the winter roads. Lucy, although she was younger, had seemed the elder and more responsible then. As they grew older there had been pranks in which Lucy had always been the leader: getting lost, bird-nesting in some remote wood; bathing together, contrary to injunction, in the innocent indecency of childhood. David spoke of his mother's death, and his father's remarriage to the Highland housekeeper who had become Phœbe's mother. Lucy had been his boyish confidante in these difficult years. He had forgotten that no one knew so much about him. She had taken him back into another world. It was strange to be sitting now in theatrical lodgings in a great town, hearing again so many long-unheard echoes; hearing them from a sophisticated young woman whose mode of life would certainly be open to the criticism of his friends.

'But, David,' – suddenly Lucy stopped – 'I quite forgot I read last week that you were engaged to be married!'

David had forgotten, too.

'Tell me about her.'

David told her about Grace. Who she was. How he had come to know her. As he told her, he found himself wondering why Lucy should be putting so many questions, watching him so closely.

'She sounds to me just the very wife for you,' she said at length.

'I must have thought so, too, when I asked her to marry me.' David laughed. Yet the disloyal overtones of his joke seemed wrong somehow.

'She's a lucky girl, David.'

'Thank you, Lucy.'

'No. I mean it.'

But the carefree atmosphere of this meeting had changed. It was no more pleasantly intimate, innocently clandestine. She saw that David was ill at ease, and, now that their meal was at an end, she was not surprised that he should remember some duty and plead that he must be gone.

'Of course, David. It was kind of you to stay so long, to talk about old times.' She watched him get himself into his overcoat in the little dim entrance hall, and waved him goodbye as he turned downward out of sight on the gaslit stone staircase.

III

In the two hours or so that David had spent in Lucy's rooms the weather had grown colder. As he made his way down Hill Street he found himself slipping in ruts of frozen snow. Above him the sky was clear and there were stars.

He wondered now why he had so suddenly invented an excuse to leave Lucy. It had been a queer little visit, he told himself, smiling into the darkness, and one that for all its unusualness had done no one any harm. It had been pleasant to recall the past with someone who had once been a playmate; to laugh at little, long-forgotten things.

He thought of the odd, friendly room where he had found Lucy, and of Lucy herself. The little pinafored girl had turned

147

into a creature of much charm. She had easiness of manners, quickness of wit, tact – all accomplishments that David valued highly. There was something gallant about her independence.

Presently he found himself at the foot of the hill pondering which way he should take. He wondered now that he did not feel tired, as he had done earlier in the evening. It had been a strange day. Lunch with the Dermotts. Robert Dermott's too generous offer. Grace's formal visit to Grosvenor Terrace. And then, this unexpected visit to Lucy. Now his day was done. He could go home, write a letter to the girl he was to marry, and rest. But somehow he was restless. As though there were an important question forming itself in the hidden places of his mind. A troublesome question that would sooner or later take shape, rise to the surface, and have to be answered.

The air was crisp and frosty. It was pleasant and refreshing. He would walk about the lighted City to stretch his legs and think. This decision taken, he pushed on hurriedly, noting very little where he went. Now his thoughts were taking him back to his boyhood at the Laigh Farm. He had been the youngest. His sisters had petted him when he was little. They had laughed at his natural gentilities and encouraged him in them for their own amusements. His mother had made as much of him as was possible to a busy farmer's wife. Childish pictures rose before him – things that had not crossed his mind for years. A secret clearing in the wood that he had called his kingdom. A cave by the river's edge that he had always hurried past because of the giant who lived there. A pond rimmed with bulrushes and yellow irises, where the prince of all the frogs lived. The imaginings of an ordinary, sensitive child, set alight from the few picture-books that had found their way to the children of the Laigh Farm. He had not told his brothers and sisters about these things. He had shrunk from their laughter. But he had always told the little girl, as together they clattered stockily along the road to school. Lucy was quick in the uptake, and could be depended upon not to laugh in scorn.

Jets were being turned out on the long brass gas-pipes in the shop-windows as David made his way down into the centre of the town. Shutters were going up. In front of one or two shops the pavement was being swept clean of snow, and ashes thrown down. In Renfield Street horses were straining uphill with their loads, clapping their labouring hoofs on the sanded track and puffing jets of steam into the frosty air. On the steeper parts of the hill the brakes of descending tramcars were screaming.

Why this muffled excitement? Was it

because he must tell Arthur of Robert Dermott's offer? Or was it over-sensitive of him to worry lest he should seem ungrateful to the brother who had done so much for him?

David was perplexed. The world had been too good to him. He had nothing to complain of. And now it looked as though by the mere fact of having chosen a gentle and desirable girl to be his wife, a fortune was to be handed to him. Why, then, this inward dispeace? For one strange moment he had an impulse to turn back to Lucy Rennie's lodging; to ask her as an old friend what was the matter with him. No; that was ridiculous. Whatever she had been to him as a child, she was, to all intents, a stranger to him now.

Without noting what he did, he had come down as far as the Clyde. He was crossing Glasgow Bridge. The lamps on the balustrade on either side stood up like pale jewels, strung out against the glowing darkness. The tide was in. On the right he could distinguish the gilded figurehead of a clipper. In the river further down there were dim shapes of masts, and moving lights. At the far end of the bridge he turned into the Georgian quiet of Carlton Place. Here there was a sudden peace, an absence of traffic.

Was this marriage he was making just an impetuous mistake? Had he rushed into it unnecessarily? He remembered how, not so

150

many weeks ago, he had raged along the night streets on his way home, inflamed by Irving's Hamlet, thinking excited thoughts even as he was doing now. Was it all a mistake, then? It couldn't be. What of the feeling of emptiness, of all the sorrow of a young man's loneliness that he had felt on that night? Was he not far better now?

He was in the traffic again, crossing the Stockwell Bridge. The river stood full and high beneath it, sending up slow, zigzag reflections from its black, glassy surface. Now he was in the bright rabble of the Stockwell itself. Even on this cold night there were barefoot children. There was laughter and drunkenness, misery and rough good cheer. There were barrows with flares set above them. By one of these a powerful Irishwoman with raven hair, gipsy ear-rings and harsh, weatherbeaten good looks, called, 'Rosy apples'. She picked up an apple, breathed upon it, and quickly rubbing it on her apron, held it out to David. Hungry urchins stood gazing up, their faces white in the light of her flare. Further on, a second woman, leading a donkey-cart, was calling, 'Caller herring'. A cold trade on such a night. An old man standing at the kerb kept muttering quickly, 'A penny, a penny,' to no one in particular. David saw that he was selling cotton pocket-handkerchiefs. The doorman, in splendid gold braid, was ordering ragged, half-grown boys from the lighted entrance of the Scotia Music Hall. They were shouting back obscene impertinence. A locomotive on the viaduct overhead puffed out a fountain of steam and red ashes, making a display of fireworks against the night.

David found himself making in the direction of home; pounding along, his feet crackling the frozen snow as he went. He had some distance to go, but he did not think of this. There was bright moonlight now. That made it easy to cut quickly through quiet sidestreets.

What was this, then, that had taken hold of him? What did he expect of himself? Was he to go to Grace and tell her that, after all, their engagement had been hasty and foolish. That was unthinkable; an idea that could not be taken seriously. And yet, here he was, striding along as though this very thought had taken upon itself a horrid shape and was following in the darkness behind him. Everything within him shrank away from the pain that such an avowal must cause. To say such a thing to Grace? Never!

The mere thought of that had, for a time, quickened still more his pace, but now at length he began to feel exhausted. He looked about him. In ten minutes more he would be home. Since he had left Lucy Rennie's rooms he had tramped down the hill, made a circle of the inner City, then walked some miles west without noticing. This was senseless. He must not let himself become so overwrought.

He took out his latch-key at the top of his stairs and let himself in. His sitting-room had been warmed by the fire that was now burning low. He held a taper to the gas, then looked about him. Here was a bleak, bachelor sort of room. There were none of the absurd, frivolous knick-knacks that made Lucy Rennie's lodging so cheerful. He threw off his overcoat and drew a chair to the fire. His feet were beginning to ache. He pulled off his boots slowly and held out the soles of his feet, one after the other, to the fire. The familiar surroundings were beginning to calm him. After a little while he even felt drowsy. The clock on his mantelshelf struck eleven. He had no idea it was so late. Better go to bed. Surely, after all this walking he would get some sleep.

Chapter Twelve

Grace Dermott had put the Moorhouse clan in her pocket. That a daughter of success should at once command the respect of a homely family in this city, where material prosperity was the common yardstick, is not, perhaps, a matter for wonder. Grace had gained everything by her engagement to David. She was beginning to have a life of her own. Hitherto she had spent her time as a pleasant, timid absorber of shocks. Between the personalities of her parents, when their strong wills threatened to clash together. Between her mother and the members of her mother's committees. Between her parents and the servants. Between one servant and another. Spasmodically, she had made the pretence of having interests of her own – working in Berlin wool; painting on china; and even, once, going the length of taking lessons on the guitar. But too often she had felt in her heart, as many a rich young woman of her time felt, that her days were gapingly, needlessly empty.

Now all this was changed. David and his family were everything. Before many mornings she was back in the carriage at Grosvenor Terrace to see how Bel's cold was getting on, ladened with conservatory grapes and flowers. She had just dropped in on her way to town, she said. Taken unawares and informally, Bel's conventionality had no choice but to break down. Grace was quite simple and direct. It was plain she had come back so soon because she liked everybody, and was making haste to know them better. She got to know Bel's children, and offered to take the two elder ones, Arthur and Isabel, to Hengler's Circus. She promised little Thomas, who was scarcely four, and who showed immediate displeasure at being left out of the party, that she would take him to Aladdin's Cavern at the Argyle House, where Aladdin would give him a toy all to himself.

Even Phœbe was forced to respond. Grace remembered the Highland woman and her children in the coach-house. The man, Phœbe told her, had left hospital and was with them now. Grace asked to be taken to see them. She stayed with them talking for some time. Phœbe could see that she was used to such people, hurting none of their quick pride with a sympathy that was blunt or heavy-handed. Grace Dermott was not, after all, perhaps, the sweet-faced nonentity Phœbe had taken her to be.

Returned from the coach-house, Grace gave Bel her hand and said she must be gone, as she wanted to look in on Sophia. Bel said goodbye with apprehension, wondering what kind of confusion she would find at Rosebery Terrace. If she had known, her apprehension would have been greater. The entire Butter family were at home. Wil and Margy had been given a skating holiday from school, and were clamouring noisily for an early meal, as they wanted to go off to skate.

Sophia was fussing round in the steam of cooking, wearing one of her little maid's aprons. 'Be quiet, children! I am being as

155

quick as ever I can. Margy, go and lay the table. Katie, did you forget we needed salt? It's too silly having no salt in the house. Wait. Here's some salt spilt on a dresser shelf. I'll scrape it together and use that. Wil, there's the bell, dear. Go and answer it. Katie's busy.'

The door was opened to Grace by a lanky boy of fifteen with some of the Moorhouse good looks. He looked at the smart young lady in the fur jacket, then at the carriage behind her, and waited, saying nothing.

Grace smiled. 'Are you Wil Butter? I'm your new Aunt Grace. Can I come in?'

A sheepish grin spread on Wil's face. He opened the door wider, and Grace followed him. 'I'll get Mother,' was all he said, leaving her standing in the hall. A moment later she heard voices, presumably in the kitchen.

'Mother, that's Aunt Grace.'

'Aunt who?'

'Grace. Uncle David's young lady.'

'Dear me! Run and tell her I'm coming. Where have you put her?'

'Nowhere.'

'Silly boy. Why didn't you show her in beside Father? I must come at once.' Sophia came into view undoing the apron. 'Grace dear, I'm delighted to see you! I'm hurrying up dinner because the children want to skate. They're so impatient. It's awful! Do come in where it's warm. William, this is Grace. This is my husband.'

A black, hairy man was sitting in the stuffy little parlour in an embroidered smoking-cap and slippers, reading the newspapers. He got up ponderously and gave Grace his hand.

As he did not offer a remark, Grace said it was very cold. Sophia said it was indeed cold, and please to sit down and warm herself.

'I only looked in to leave a brace of pheasants. Mother said she thought you might like them.'

Nothing pleased Sophia better than to receive something for nothing. 'Oh, how kind of you, dear! What a nice present!'

The dinner-bell clanged harshly. 'Oh, there's the bell. Grace, stay and have something. We all want to see you.' The words were out of Sophia's mouth before she could take them back.

So Grace sent the carriage away, and stayed to eat shepherd's pie and mashed turnips from cracked dishes laid on a stained table-cloth. Her hirsute host was expressionless and speechless, but, Grace decided, not antagonistic. With Sophia and her constant talk, flowing rather from the lack of ideas than from the possession of them, Grace was already familiar. But she was interested in the two untidy, handsome children. Like herself, they were direct and friendly, and prepared to make her one of themselves.

157

And so, this most unlikely of luncheon-parties was a success. Grace said goodbye to William and Sophia in a cloud of goodwill. The pheasants, still lying in the hall, had been duly admired, and Grace drove off towards the fog-threatened city accompanied by Wil and Margy muffled up and carrying their skates. She had undertaken to drop them at St. Vincent Pond, which was, like so many other ponds in and about the city, being advertised as having its ice in prime condition.

In the carriage she extracted a promise from them to come down to spend the day at Aucheneame on Saturday. Their Uncle David would be there, and, if it was still freezing, they would all go skating on one of the lochs in the Kilpatrick Hills. By that time the ice would be safe even on deep water.

As they sat fitting on their skates, the Butter children agreed with each other that their new aunt was a bit fussy, perhaps, but not too bad. And that they had expected their la-di-da Uncle David would want to marry more of a fool.

II

Since her first visit to Bel, two days before, Grace had not seen David. But this morning she had received a letter from him telling

158

her that he had consulted Arthur about quitting the family business in the Candleriggs, and that all was well. She had replied by electric telegram bidding David come down to Aucheneame for the night, if possible, in order to talk things over. He would find Grace at his sister Mary's house at Albany Place where she had been invited to take tea. They could drive back together.

Having left the two Butter children at St. Vincent Pond, Grace spent the intervening time shopping. In spite of the cold and the threat of fog, she went about the town with a light heart. The shops were warm, and gay with Christmas tinsel, and Miss Dermott of Aucheneame was a welcome customer. Several times Grace found herself humming little snatches from sheer pleasure, as she trod the wintry pavements, stopping every now and then to examine the contents of a window. In the light of her own happiness, the Moorhouse family seemed a grand lot. The Grosvenor Terrace household. Sophia's family. She was glad that half-grown boy and girl, who had driven part of the way into town with her, were to be her nephew and niece. Their gawky eagerness warmed her. She wondered how they were getting on with their skating, and found herself wishing she were with them. But there was this visit to be paid to Mary, where she was to see the McNairn nephews and nieces. Yes;

159

she liked the Moorhouses.

And at the centre of them all was David.

And now presently it was time to meet the carriage and make her way west once more. This time in the direction of Charing Cross and Crescents.

III

Baillie George McNairn had pompously announced this morning at breakfast that he was coming home specially to do the honours at tea. The occasion, he said, demanded it. His new sister-in-law must be received with all respect. If Grace had not been the daughter of one of Glasgow's shipping princes, if she had been the mere daughter of an empty purse, the baillie might not have felt so strongly the compulsions of politeness. But at all events, there he was with his wife, ready to receive the child of Robert Dermott with every manifestation of decorous approval.

As Grace appeared in the doorway of the snug, over-furnished drawing-room in Albany Place, it was George, plump and imposing, who advanced heavily to meet her. 'Come away, my dear, come away. Very pleased indeed.'

George did not make the reasons for his pleasure more precise, but it was nice for

160

Grace to know the mood of her host and hostess. She advanced to Mary, and was received with calm affection, remarked how foggy it was becoming, and was bidden to sit close to the fire.

For once, Grace found herself doing most of the talking. Didn't they think it unusually cold for early winter? Did they think the fog would really settle down? Wouldn't it really be a pity if it were a cold winter, when there was so much distress about? It was hard going. She was almost grateful to George when, cutting in upon her own somewhat forced efforts, he began a long panegyric on the merits of her own father, on his great brilliance as a man of business and as a leader of men. It was embarrassing to listen to, perhaps. Especially as George had so many of his facts wrong. But at least it was less of an effort than having to pump out conversation on her own account.

'And to think that he rose from nothing – nothing at all!' George was winding up his discourse on a note that a quicker, less well-disposed daughter might have found necessary for her father's sake, to qualify, when two very fat little girls of four or thereby, in much-starched white dresses, large red sashes and red buttoned boots, were pushed into the room by a hand that did not belong to any discernible body.

'Come along and see your Aunt Grace,'

161

Mary said placidly, without getting up to bring them.

'What little darlings!' Grace exclaimed.

The darlings were very slow in coming to be presented. The tea-table, groaning with every kind of cake, rich and ornamental, lay across their path, and drew their interest much more surely than any aunt, however agreeable, that they were ever likely to acquire.

Grace went to them and knelt down before them. 'What are your names?' she asked.

'Anne,' said one. 'Polly,' said the other. They both then turned away and went on examining the tea-table. They were both exactly alike, fat and round-faced, with hair cut close, like little boys. Both were so intent upon the glories to come, that Grace burst out laughing.

Their parents smiled benignly. If Grace had not been a daughter of the exalted, they might have wondered what she was laughing at.

Presently tea arrived, and with it the two elder children of the family. Georgie Mc-Nairn was fourteen, and, in so far as a beardless boy can look like a fat, middle-aged man of forty-three, George's rather heavy, undistinguished features resembled his father's. Jackie, a boy of eleven, was, on the other hand, a thin distinguished child whose features seemed entirely Moorhouse.

Like their Butter cousins, they had been skating. It did not take Grace very long to guess that they had been commanded by their father to come home in time to meet her, and that this had not pleased them very much. To put herself into their good graces, she invited them to come on Saturday with the Butters to Aucheneame.

Their parents were pleased about this, and accepted for them willingly. As George said to Mary after Grace was gone, you never knew what visits to places like Aucheneame might lead to. Mary was too lazy to bother thinking out what her husband meant. But, somehow, it would have pleased her better if her own children had been invited by themselves, and not together with Sophia's quicker-witted son and daughter.

But Grace's visit was a great success. During tea, the baillie's tongue was loosened enough to tell her at length about a long and intricate misunderstanding he had had with another member of the Town Council. His narrative was, perhaps, difficult to follow, interrupted as it was by the clatter of tea-things, the constant cross-talk of the children, the continual necessity of passing cakes to them, and of refusing cake herself. But from it all Grace understood enough to grasp that George's sound common sense had triumphed; that if it had not been for Baillie McNairn, the entire civic policy of the City of Glasgow would have taken the wrong turning. She therefore did her best to show approval at the right moments, and, when he had finished, to tell him how fortunate it was that he had been there to arrange everything so wisely.

The cup of even George's vanity was full. David, when he arrived, was surprised at the amount of joviality that his stiff and humourless brother-in-law was displaying. He was even more surprised when, as Grace and he rose to say goodbye, George slapped him on the back, and told him that there wasn't another girl in the West of Scotland that he would prefer as a sister-in-law.

IV

'Well, David, are you pleased to see me?' Grace and David, buried in rugs, were settling themselves for the long, cold drive to Aucheneame.

For reply, David turned to Grace and kissed her. She had looked forward to having him in the carriage all to herself. She took one of his hands and drew it inside her muff.

At the McNairns', David had seemed unusually solemn. It was a mood she did not yet know. 'Are you all right, David?'

'Of course. Why?'

'Oh, nothing.' She must not be a fussy wife.

Men, she had read somewhere, detested that above all things. Yet she imagined he had looked preoccupied, and even a little strained, as he had come into Mary's drawing-room. But David was so much in her thoughts, that she was over-quick to imagine things about him.

'Tell me about Arthur, David,' she said.

'Oh, Arthur was very good.' He told her about his interview with his brother. How Arthur had expressed his pleasure that David should have such good fortune. He had made no difficulty whatever about David's going. Trade was bad, and the slackness of the times made it easier. David had promised to remain until the end of the year, when he would be ready to come into Dermott Ships.

There was animated talk about all this. Grace was pleased to see that, as David sat talking to her, the sense of strain seemed to go from him. Her presence seemed to soothe him. The shadow of the cloud that had crossed her happiness passed over and was gone. David was himself again. And more affectionate than ever he had been. With the affection, somehow, of a child. This again was a new mood, but not one to trouble her.

She told him of her visits to the family. How she had seen Phœbe's Highlanders. Her unexpected lunch with Sophia. How she had invited the children to skate at the weekend. They laughed together over this and that. The impatience of the Butter children. The comic appearance of Mary's little twin girls.

Presently, after a pause in their talk, he turned to look at her. 'Grace,' he asked, 'when are we to be married?'

She felt the colour rising in her cheeks. It was the first time he had asked this of her.

'Do you want to be married soon, David?'

'Yes. As soon as ever we can.'

'It won't be long, my darling.' She had dropped her voice to a whisper. She wished that she were clever, that she could read the mind of this man who was all the world to her. Something told her it had not been a conventional lover's question. There were unmistakable overtones of appeal in his voice, overtones that baffled her. She wished she knew what he meant. She wanted to talk about it. To ask him why. But what could a brotherless, cloistered young woman know about the make-up of men?

He was sitting now, looking before him in the dusk of the carriage. Grace could not see his face distinctly enough to tell if the look of strain had come back. But something told her it was there. Instinct prompted her next words.

'We would be happy and safe if we were married, wouldn't we, David?'

'Yes, Grace. We would be safe.'

The hand she had drawn inside her muff grasped her own hand tightly. It was time for them to get down before its grip was relaxed.

Chapter Thirteen

It was in the morning of the last day of the year, a Tuesday. Margaret Ruanthorpe-Moorhouse had written to Grace Dermott inviting her to spend New Year with them, along with David. It was disgraceful, her letter had said, that all the rest of the family should be getting to know her so well, while she and Mungo, marooned as they were in Ayrshire, had not yet met her. Could they come on the Saturday before New Year and spend a week, or the better part of it? Phœbe, who was a favourite with her mother, Lady Ruanthorpe, was coming to Duntrafford House, with Henry Hayburn. Together, they would all make a pleasant New Year party.

Grace showed herself loath to leave her own parents at this time. It would, she protested, be her last unmarried New Year with them. On being scolded by Mrs. Dermott, however, for working up a deal of sentimentality about nothing, and reminded that her first duty was to her man, Grace gave way at once. It would give her great pleasure, she wrote, to come to the Duntrafford Dower House to get to know everybody and to see David's calf country.

But David and Grace were prevented from going down into Ayrshire on the day arranged. To add to the poverty and the evil times, the year 1878 closed with a bitter frost lasting four weeks, the longest period the West of Scotland – a region of wet, southwest winds – had known for twenty years. In the poorest quarters of the city the suffering was intense. But those who were young and had some money spent all their leisure perfecting their skating. Local trains were filled with cheerful young people making their way to nearby lochs and ponds. Such places, lighted late into the night, and provided with coffee-stalls, were being advertised among the places of entertainment in the daily papers together with the pantomimes, Hengler's Circus, the musichalls and the demonstrations of Pepper's Ghost at the Coal Exchange.

On the Friday after Christmas, however, there were heavy snowfalls up and down the country. To begin with, long-distance trains could not come through. Then even local traffic came to a standstill. On Saturday night the west wind brought the rain in torrents. Sunday was a day of flooding and confusion. By Monday communications were beginning to reopen. The snow was being washed away. On Monday evening David and Grace, accompanied by Phœbe and Henry, reached Duntrafford.

Now this following morning Grace was standing with Margaret, waving to David as he drove off with Mungo in the pony-trap. Mungo had his usual business at the Laigh Farm, and Margaret had instructed him, when that was finished, to drive across to Greenhead to find out if Miss Rennie were there. She had not forgotten Lucy Rennie's kindness to her in the train. Remembering that she would be at Greenhead over New Year, she was sending a note asking Miss Rennie to come to see her.

'Have you met this Rennie girl?' Margaret asked Grace as they set off on foot to Duntrafford House, where Grace was to be presented to Sir Charles and Lady Ruanthorpe.

Grace had not yet met Miss Rennie.

'You would be surprised if you knew her people. Very ordinary farm folks. Not that there is anything extraordinary about that,' Margaret hastened to say, remembering, perhaps, her own husband. 'But Lucy Rennie herself has turned into something so very different. She might be an English-woman. You would never guess she was an Ayrshire farmer's daughter.'

Grace expressed her interest in Miss Rennie. She had, Grace understood, spent a long time in London, and no doubt that accounted for the change which had taken place.

Margaret said, 'No doubt.' And they walked on in the direction of the Big House in silence.

Grace wondered about Margaret herself. She belonged to a type with whom the Dermotts, as yet, had little contact. Robert Dermott's fortune had put him among the locally important. He lived in a large house in a country place, and allowed himself servants, and, when he could, a country life. But he and his kind were not yet of the county. The industrial great of Scotland had not yet, to any extent, taken to educating their children in England, thus levelling their manners, their speech and their habits of thought with their like across the border, as would happen a generation later. They had not yet begun to mould them to the English county-squire pattern.

And thus, Sir Charles Ruanthorpe, an Englishman, with his lady and daughter, seemed as different to Grace Dermott as an American might have seemed. Their controlled good manners. Their English accent and turn of speech. Their habit of distinguished understatement. Their large hospitality, which was, unlike Scottish hospitality, never pressed. Their sureness of their own point of view. Their quick responsibility for their dependents. They belonged to a world that was trained to authority. She did not define these things, but she felt them, and like many another who uses the English language but does not possess English blood, she had to adjust. But their goodwill was unmistakable. So, quick to blame herself for any lack of warm feelings, Grace decided that Mungo's wife and her parents were everything that was admirable.

But how Mungo Moorhouse, an Ayrshire farmer, had come to marry Margaret Ruanthorpe was a mystery to her. How these so seemingly different people had come to make a match of it was beyond her understanding. She must get David to tell her, when she had him to herself.

II

It was many years since David Moorhouse had found himself in Ayrshire for any length of time. He had not made a stay even of four days, as he was now doing, for quite ten years. As he sat beside Mungo, looking about him, this came to his mind. It struck him as odd. There had been nothing much to bring him back to the Laigh Farm house, he supposed. Mungo's bachelor existence had been all work and no play. To a young man who had welcomed the town and its ways,

171

the farm had little attraction. Even before
the accident that had ended the lives of his
father and stepmother, he had come home
very little. Where Arthur was, there was
David's anchorage.

But now it was pleasant to be driving in
country that was stamped on his first
memories. He was surprised at his quick
familiarity with the twists of the muddy
lanes, the gates and thorn hedges, the
clumps of high trees on the round hill-tops,
the shape of the green, rolling fields. They
were there as he remembered them. This
midwinter Ayrshire had its own beauty. The
torrents of rain at the weekend had washed
the fields clear of snow. It lay now only
where there had been deep drifts, sodden
and stained with red mud. In contrast, the
wet fields seemed in the morning sunshine
to have taken on a greenness that gave them,
almost, the freshness of spring. Furrows and
ditches were full. Streams were raging
torrents. The placid River Ayr, as they
crossed the bridge, had run wild, and was
dashing itself against the sandstone cliffs – a
boiling, red-brown cataract. There was a
newness, a promise about this Ayrshire of
the Winter Solstice; a purging, a washing of
the fertile lands, that again in proper season
they should be clean and waiting to receive
the seed and bear the annual harvest.

David, alert just now, and oddly sensitive

to impression, had eyes for everything. His mind, unsettled and quick, kept darting hither and thither. Why did he find himself so much uplifted by the country this morning? It was said that as you grew older you began to put back your roots – try to touch back to your beginnings. Now he was approaching middle age. Perhaps these feelings were beginning to awake in himself. He must come to Ayrshire more often. No. They must come. He and Grace. He had been unhappy and restless in the last weeks. So unhappy and restless that he had even mentioned it to Bel. But she had given him to understand that, in her opinion, this was what being in love did to a man. That when at length he held his wife in his arms, his unhappiness would be resolved, his body and mind would find their assuagement and their peace.

Well, it would come soon. At the beginning of March. Neither of them wanted a fuss, but, when it came to the point, a fuss there would no doubt be. If it were merely as an exhibition of Mrs. Dermott's organising talent.

There was the Laigh Farm now, over there, with the high trees in the stack-yard. There were still rooks' nests in the upper branches. They had all been born at the Laigh – all the Moorhouse brothers and sisters. And that was the road-end where he

173

had been used to meet Lucy Rennie on the way to school. They had cut part of the wood there, further down where they had gathered wild hyacinths in the springtime. The Bluebell Wood, they had called it.

Lucy Rennie. Mungo, who was busy, had asked David to set him down at the Laigh Farm and drive over alone with Margaret's message. She would be glad to see Lucy at any time. But – and David was to put this tactfully – Lady Ruanthorpe had suggested that Lucy might come across to the Big House, dine with them on New Year's night, and sing to them all. He was to put it that they knew this was asking much of a professional musician, and of a daughter who was so little at home; but that it would be giving great pleasure to two old people who had no other means of hearing real music.

As they turned into the yard of the Laigh Farm, Phœbe and Henry Hayburn appeared at the back door of the farmhouse.

'Hullo, what are you doing here?' David shouted.

Phœbe shouted back, 'Showing Henry round.'

'Did you walk across?'

'Yes.'

'You must have come early.'

Mungo was jumping down. His two old collies, Nith and Doon, rushed out to meet him. The old ploughman who had been promoted to be farm grieve came out. He spied David and called to him by name.

'Oh, it's you that's up there, Davie? How's yersel'?'

'Fine, James. How are you?'

'Fine, Davie. Man, yer a great stranger! Are ye no' comin' in?'

'I'm going up to Greenhead. I'll come in when I come back.'

A sudden mood had taken David. He wanted to be away from it all. This place was a memory, with his mother and father, his sisters and brothers, all of them there. Its present reality offended him. The stones had no right to be standing any longer. It should have no existence but as an image in his mind. That shed was new. It didn't belong. That door was the wrong colour and had hinges he didn't know. They had made a new window in that wall. These things didn't really exist. They were not to be found in the records of his mind. For so many years he had turned a snobbish, adolescent back on the Laigh Farm. Now it must be taking its revenge.

He took the reins from Mungo a little un-certainly. He had not driven a horse for many years.

'Wait a minute. We'll come with you. Come on, Henry.'

Phœbe and Henry were up beside him. For some reason undefinable, his heart became lighter. He was glad they were coming to Greenhead too.

III

Lucy Rennie also had been going through the experience of coming back. This experience, indeed, was sharper than David's, because she had left her home in Ayrshire as a rebel. Now her father and elder sister were treating her with as much forbearance and tact as their peasant manners would allow them. But she did not like being treated as a brand snatched from the burning. If she had been a little scorched, and if she chose to risk being scorched again, that was her own affair. Yet she could not but be touched at the anxiety of her family to please.

She was sitting in the best room of the farmhouse – a stiff, red-plush room, seldom used, that had been dusted and warmed against her coming – when her sister Jessie, a stocky country woman, came to tell her that Davie Moorhouse of the Laigh was there with his sister and a young man. They were talking to her father in the stack-yard. Lucy roused herself, went downstairs, and out by the farmyard door. Advancing across the yard, she made an incongruous figure as she held up her elegant skirts to avoid the mud and the puddles. When she came within speaking distance, she called to draw their attention.

'Good morning. Why aren't you coming in?'

'We're only here for a minute or two. It's just to deliver a message. Your father has asked us in already,' David shouted.

Old Tom Rennie, squat and graceless, grunted assent.

She had a moment more before she came up to them. David was standing hatless in his dark clothes. His sister was standing beside him, bareheaded too. Where had these Moorhouses got their good looks? The morning sun was striking down on David's warm chestnut hair and his long, distinguished face. Phœbe's black hair was wind-blown and untidy, but her cheeks, were glowing. And, as everybody must, Lucy marvelled at her strange, Highland eyes. They might have stepped out of Raeburn canvasses, both of them.

'So that's what little Phœbe Moorhouse grew into!' she said, holding out her hand admiringly.

Phœbe did not attempt to make any easy reply to this. She merely gave Lucy her own hand in return.

Lucy turned to the second young man. He was wearing country tweeds in a large trellis check. His thin, bony body was buttoned up in a tight, shapeless jacket, and his long legs were in narrow trousers. He took off a hat of the same cloth with a skip back and front. He seemed a pleasant, pug-nosed sort of creature, and bestowed upon Lucy a boyish smile. David introduced him as Henry Hayburn, a future brother-in-law.

'You are a very lucky young man, Mr. Hayburn.' She looked towards Phœbe, who had turned aside to pat the nose of a cart-horse that had put his head over the fence.

Henry grinned, and went to join old Tom Rennie, who was on his way across to Phœbe.

'And how are you this morning, David?' Lucy asked, giving him her hand. She wondered why the colour had flooded up over David's face, why he looked at her as though she were hiding something from him. He had not been like this when he had called on her in Glasgow.

'Oh, I'm all right, thank you.'

Why was he embarrassed? There were men, she knew, who could not talk to a young woman like herself without immediately becoming conscious of her sex. But she never would have guessed that David Moorhouse might turn into one of these.

As he stood giving her his message, Lucy wondered. After all, within his own narrow range, he was rather a sophisticated young man. What, then, was there about her to embarrass him?

Yes, she told David, she would be glad to

visit Mrs. Ruanthorpe-Moorhouse. No, she was doing nothing this afternoon, and would be glad to come across for tea. It was very kind of Mrs. Ruanthorpe-Moorhouse to ask her sister too. She would tell her, but she did not think she would be likely to come. The Duntraffords would readily understand that Jessie's duties at the farm would not allow it. When David and the others had gone, Lucy picked her elegant way back across the farmyard smiling with satisfaction. Her stay at Greenhead, then, was not to be so dull, after all. At their mid-day meal she was pleased to see that her father and sister seemed glad that the Big House should be taking notice of her. Here was her achievement in terms that they could understand. For in those days, the landlord, if he had any sort of dignity, was still held in honour, and regarded with some awe by his tenants.

Lucy looked forward to her visit to Dun-trafford with pleasure and no sense of shyness. There was nothing to overawe her about Margaret Ruanthorpe-Moorhouse, and just as little, really, about old Sir Charles and his wife. Did she not, after all, earn much of her living teaching the daughters, and singing in the drawing-rooms, of personages much more important than they?

179

Chapter Fourteen

Grace had looked forward with pleasure to meeting the remarkable Miss Rennie. From everything Margaret had said, she seemed an unusual young woman. This afternoon she would see this farmer's daughter who had disappeared from her home and re-appeared a polished, accomplished and independent young lady.

And yet, when Grace came to look back on this visit to Duntrafford, it was clear that things had begun to go wrong for her on the afternoon of Lucy Rennie's call at the Dower House. It was difficult to tell just in what respect the savour had gone out of things. Grace was not a worldly person, neither was she particularly quick-witted, nor, least of all, had this gentle daughter of indulgence had cause in her life to learn the cruelties of jealousy. But she was head over heels in love with the man she was to marry, and her tenderness towards him was open to every wind that blew across it.

Miss Rennie came. And Miss Rennie was charming. Miss Rennie was quite obviously enjoying herself.

Lucy, sitting in the midst of stiff respect-

180

ability, and pleasantly friendly – but very definite – condescension, found herself being given tea by the laird's daughter. Yet, from Margaret's manner to her, she was made to feel that, whatever she did with herself she would never rise to the level of the Ruanthorpes. And here was Mungo Moorhouse of the Laigh, safely high and dry, and out of the struggle, having joined his blood to the blood of the Big House. And these young people. So very much now the children of privilege, all of them. They were all very sure of their complacent, northern world. There was just enough of the street arab in Lucy to see the fun of it all. She had known the artist quarter of a Paris that was settling down after the Prussian occupation. There, respectability, she remembered, had been so very much a matter of ready cash. It had been as fragile a thing as that. And as for the airs the Ruanthorpes gave themselves, she was accustomed to sing in houses of people of vastly greater importance; to rub shoulders with snobs who would have looked down their noses at old Sir Charles and his lady.

But she liked David. And he seemed to like her. From her memory of him, he had been a gentle, but rather self-possessed little boy. She had wondered this morning at his obvious confusion when he spoke to her. It was the same again this afternoon. What did he think of this sweet, rather limp young woman

181

he was going to marry. Why had he chosen her? But of course! She was rolling in money, and David was, after all, a Moorhouse. And quite right, too. Money perhaps wasn't everything. But, look at it as you would, it lifted you up, out of the battle. She dared say David would do very well with Miss Dermott.

David had come to her side. She turned to him.

'I heard Margaret speaking to you about dinner tomorrow,' he said.

'Yes, I'm coming. It was very kind of Lady Ruanthorpe to ask me.'

'I'm glad. We'll all be there. I hope you're going to sing.'

'Of course. If they want me to. What kind of songs do you like?'

'I'm not particularly musical.'

'But you must like some songs. All men do. If they know no other kind, they say they like simple, old-fashioned songs.'

'I think these are the kind I *do* like.'

'Oh, David! David!'

Grace, who was near enough to hear this conversation, wondered what there was in all this to cause Miss Rennie's laughter.

'Do you never sing simple, old-fashioned songs?' she heard David asking.

'Of course. A great many of them. I sing for my living.'

No, Grace Dermott did not like Lucy Rennie. She seemed to be able to play on that instrument which was David Moorhouse, to strike notes that she, the owner of the instrument, was unable to touch. Miss Rennie was quick and gay, and had a mass of small talk. She was not superficially vulgar. She was neither loud-voiced nor pushing. Her behaviour was perfect. But Grace, too, had noticed David's changing colour, his betrayal of dispeace in Lucy Rennie's presence. She was glad when Miss Rennie rose to go.

On the doorstep, when they had waved Lucy out of sight, Grace turned from the others to David.

'How warm it is. And moonlight! Come for five minutes' walk. Just as we are.'

They sauntered arm in arm through the Duntrafford shrubberies. The moonshine was making silver and black velvet of the shining path and the wet leaves of the deep rhododendron bushes. They found themselves at a viewpoint on the cliffs looking far down on a sharp bend of the river Ayr. There was a churning eddy where the flood was forced to change its course. The moon had caught the water where it boiled. They could see the angry river emerge for a moment into the light of the whirlpool, turn itself into a cauldron of cold, white metal, then plunge on, roaring into the darkness. They bent over the balustrade hand in hand.

'It's wonderful, isn't it, David?'

183

'Yes. Shall we go back now?'

'Yes.'

They wandered back to the Dower House. It was Grace who kept hold of David's hand.

II

Lady Ruanthorpe's dinner-party was for ten. Herself and Sir Charles, along with the party from the Dower House, made eight of them. In addition to that there was, of course, Lucy. And, with great forethought on her own part, as the old lady considered, she had invited a shy young man who made his living as a piano-teacher among the daughters of the county. Thus, Miss Rennie would not have to accompany her own singing. The two musicians were made the guests of honour, Grace having already been given her place on the right hand of Sir Charles on the previous evening. The shrinking young man was placed on the right hand of Lady Ruanthorpe while Lucy sat to the right of Sir Charles. Though these people were mere entertainers, she saw to it that they suffered no discourtesy.

The timid young man was petrified when he saw what his position at table was to be. But a glass of sherry with his soup did wonders. And he quickly found that Lady

Ruanthorpe either did not hear, or did not pay attention to a word he said. She kept delivering a monologue at him. The songs she sang when she was a girl. What a wonderful voice her father had had. So good, indeed, that he might have been a professional singer, if he had not been a Lieutenant-General. How she had been piped into dinner, when she was staying with friends in the Highlands. How she had been staying near Glasgow, when her daughter was a little girl, and her host had pressed her to stay over to hear a pianist called Chopin. She had always regretted she had not done so, for she had since been told that his music had become famous. Was this the case? Or was she talking nonsense? Perhaps Mr. Wilkie could tell her. For a moment Mr. Wilkie emerged from the enjoyment of the best food and drink he had ever tasted, to tell her that yes, Chopin's music was quite well known.

At the other end of the table, Lucy was enjoying herself hugely. Sir Charles, she was amused to note, regarded her as something of a scarlet woman, and was determined, in so far as it could be done at the age of eighty, and under the eye of his daughter – he was safely shielded from his wife by a forest of epergnes, maidenhair, flowers and candlesticks – to prove to Miss Rennie that he, in his time, had known very well what it was to sow a wild oat or two. A mention of the fact that she knew Paris set him off on a long description of a sojourn there as a young man in his twenties, at the gay, cynical time of the Bourbon restoration. He had been sent by his parents to learn French. But he must admit, he said, looking at Lucy with a twinkle in his fierce, bloodshot eyes, that he had learnt more than French, perhaps. Lucy would fain have driven him to bay by asking him to tell her just what he *had* learnt. But this would have delighted Sir Charles too much, and might have led to talk not quite suitable for Lady Ruanthorpe's dinner-table. Besides, demureness, she kept reminding herself, must be the keynote tonight. So, when Sir Charles continued archly to mention the names of resorts of entertainment, and the names of the notorious who entertained there, Lucy found herself replying with gay innocence that she knew nothing of these places or people – as was indeed the case, for Sir Charles had known Paris fifty years before she had. But within the limits of discretion, she succeeded in keeping her host amused. So much so, indeed, that when Lady Ruanthorpe rose to take the ladies from the room, Sir Charles patted Lucy on the shoulder, said she was a capital girl; and where had her father got her? And she must come across and see them whenever she came to Greenhead. Now, immediately under the eye of Lady Ruanthorpe and the other women, Lucy smiled with becoming diffidence, thanked him very much, but rather thought it might be some time before she was back in Ayrshire.

For most of them the remainder of the evening went very pleasantly. As Lucy had guessed, old Lady Ruanthorpe had invited her much more from a feeling of self-importance than from any real desire to hear her perform. The evening was well advanced before Lady Ruanthorpe, who had been enjoying her own dinner-party far too much to remember Miss Rennie's talents, at last begged the musicians to go to the piano. A first song proved to Lucy that she could not trust the obliging young man's playing too far. But it did not matter. They were a party who would only appreciate David's 'old-fashioned, simple songs'. She had brought a number of these, and all agreed that she sang them charmingly. Especially Sir Charles, who had talked steadily during the performance of each of them. But everyone was pleased, complimented her, and was friendly. For a moment, later in the evening, she found herself beside Grace who, fearful of showing her dislike, set herself to praise Lucy's singing. Lucy was acknowledging Grace's kindness when David came across and joined them.

'Well, David! Are these songs old-fashioned and simple enough for you?'

'I thought they were beautiful. Don't you

187

like them yourself?'

'I've sung them very often.'

A servant appeared to announce that a conveyance was waiting to take Miss Rennie back to Greenhead.

'Couldn't you sing just one more song?' Grace asked.

'A song that you really like this time!' David said.

Lucy went to the piano. With a friendly nod to the pianist, saying she hadn't the music, but thought she could remember, she sat down and played and sang. It was a gentle nostalgic sort of song in a foreign language. But it was evident that she loved this music, and her voice was warm. When it was over she swung round in the stool to find David immediately behind her. On his face there was a look of embarrassment.

'Well, David, was that too high falutin for you?'

'No.' And in a moment— 'What was it?'

'It's called *Nussbaum*, by Schumann.'

'Will you sing it again at Bel's concert?'

'Yes, if you want me to.'

Lucy said her goodbyes. And as she drove home under the stars, with the soft west wind in her face, she thought of David Moorhouse and wondered.

III

A winter sun, not yet far above the horizon, was shining bravely as Grace came down to breakfast next morning. She found Margaret alone behind the teacups. A bright fire was burning. The little dining-room of the Dower House was warm and cheerful.

'Good morning, Grace. How did you sleep? There's your porridge and ham and eggs. You'll help yourself, won't you?'

Grace was getting used to Margaret's matter-of-fact, English voice. She made everything she said, to Grace's West of Scotland ears, sound cut-and-dried and official. It was not a voice crammed with overtones of sympathy, but neither did it contain any overtones of spleen. It was the voice, Grace had decided, of a person you could depend upon; the voice of a woman who had solved her own problems quite straightforwardly. The bright sunshine and Margaret's crisp friendliness cheered Grace. She had not slept well. The New Year's party at Duntrafford House last night should have been pleasant enough, but somehow, for her at least, the evening had fallen flat. Quick to blame herself, she had lain awake in bed telling herself she was a fool. Sir Charles and Lady Ruanthorpe were old, eccentric and wilful. But they had been hospitable and kind. With the others, of course, she was

189

already on familiar terms. Surely Miss Rennie could not matter to her happiness? Or was she troubled because David had shown too much interest in Lucy? Was she, Grace, at last learning what it was to be jealous?

She had lain in bed scolding herself. She was being quite ridiculous. David had known Lucy all his life. If she was going to resent every gesture of friendliness her husband made to other women, what kind of marriage was before her? These thoughts had chased themselves round in her mind until at last she had fallen into uneasy sleep.

But now the sun was shining. And Margaret was sitting, the very picture of re-assuring normality, rapping out observations. Where the early snowdrops were to be found. How the gardeners had planted thousands of daffodils under the beech-trees of the park. How the shrubs in front needed cutting down. And now here was David himself, followed by Phœbe and Henry, all saying good morning with pink, new-washed faces, all cheerful, and making plans for the day.

'What do you mean to do with your-selves?' Margaret asked David and Grace.

David turned to Grace. 'Have you any ideas?'

'I haven't seen the Laigh Farm, you know.'

'We'll go over there.'

This was pleasant. She would have David

to herself this morning. They would drive out together on this pleasant morning, and her own unhappiness would be forgotten.

It was much as she had hoped. They drove between bare hedges by fields where ploughmen, taking advantage of the soft weather, were at work. Each team looked like the last. A pair of sleek, gigantic Clydesdales. The Argonaut's bow of the plough turning the smooth, red wave of loam. The clank of harness. The cloud of following rooks and gulls. The sturdy figure of the Ayrshire ploughman stepping steadily as he kept his furrow even – stepping in the footsteps of a great poet, who once had tilled the red Ayrshire earth not many miles from here.

David seemed pleased to tell her about familiar things as they passed. The road the brothers and sisters had taken when they went to school. The mill where their father had taken his sacks of grain. A pool in the river where he had learnt to swim. David, a working farmer's son, had known a childhood of interest and variety, such as she, the daughter of a wealthy businessman, had never known.

They found Mungo at the Laigh Farm directing his men. The old grieve was pleased to see David, and shouted to him.

'Ye said ye were comin' back the other day, Davie. But ye didna come.'

'Well, here I am now, James.'

They descended, and Grace was presented. Presently she was in the farm kitchen, so familiar to the Moorhouses, so strange to herself. She had to allow tea to be made for her by the wife of Mungo's manager as they sat in front of the great kitchen fire. She was taken round the house. She was shown the room where David had slept with Mungo before Arthur had taken him to Glasgow. Phœbe's little attic bedroom. The room David's parents had occupied after they had decided to take away the concealed bed from the kitchen. Where Mary and Sophia had slept as young girls. For David's sake, Grace was interested in everything. She tried to see the beloved ghost of a little chestnut-haired boy in these bare-scrubbed rooms.

They wandered outside. Then through the outhousing, saw this and that, and at last said their goodbyes and drove out of the farm close.

'Are we going back by another way?' Grace asked presently.

'No. Not exactly,' David said. 'Lucy Rennie left a piece of music, and I told Margaret I would take it to her.'

Grace glanced at David sideways. Jealousy rose within her like a flame. 'Why didn't you tell me we had to go to the Rennies' farm before?' she asked, keeping her voice even with an effort.

192

'I thought you knew. Is it so important?'

'No.'

'Well, then.' David drove on saying nothing further.

Grace looked at him again. The expression of his face was fixed. She turned. 'David, I don't want to go up to Greenhead Farm. After all, one piece of music can easily be posted. I want to go back to Margaret.'

'But, Grace, that's absurd. There's Greenhead just up there.'

Grace said no more. They drove up the farm road and into the Greenhead farmyard. Old Tom Rennie came out for them.

'Good morning, Mr. Rennie. I have brought some music that Lucy left behind last night,' David shouted, preparing to jump down.

'She's no here, Davie. She's away tae Ayr wi' Jessie.'

Grace saw David's face fall as he handed the old man the roll of music, said goodbye and turned his horse.

They drove back in silence. The colour seemed to have gone out of the morning. It was just a bleak, midwinter day. At Duntrafford a groom caught their horse's head, and David ran round to help Grace down. Without looking at him, she turned away and ran into the house.

Chapter Fifteen

David's world had tumbled about his ears. He had pushed the knowledge away from him. But he knew now. It was past all hiding. He was in love with Lucy Rennie.

On this, the first Monday of the year 1879, he sat, huddled over the fire in his lodgings, perplexed and miserable. He had brought Grace from Duntrafford on Saturday, taken her to Aucheneame, and spent the weekend there. Today had been his first day in Dermott Ships Limited. This morning he had travelled to town with the chairman of the company, and he had been received as though he were the chairman's son. At Aucheneame, and at the office, he had had to act the part of the happy, fortunate young man into whose lap fortune was pouring everything; not a pleasant part to play, when his senses had been surprised, and when, whatever his behaviour towards the Dermotts, he must feel a cheat and an impostor.

He wondered what Robert Dermott had thought of him in the office this morning. He had been dazed and slow. Had the old man begun to wonder if his daughter had chosen a fool for a husband? And yesterday at

194

Aucheneame. He wondered what Grace thought of him. Had she suspected anything? He did not see how she could. Yet, when he came to think of it, he had thought her manner subdued and a little aloof. And he had been too self-conscious, too self-accusing to ask if anything were troubling her.

David shivered, and picking up the poker, dangled it in his hand, thinking. The frosty weather had come back again. Outside it was very cold. Again skating was in full swing. He stirred the fire.

Grace. His mind went back and forth over the short span of the weeks of his engagement to her. From the beginning things had gone well. He was getting the habit of Grace; getting the habit of her commanding, warmhearted parents. They had turned, in that short time, into pleasant, sympathetic relatives. He was on the easiest terms with them. This had been a calculated attachment, but he had calculated well. His own measure of worldly wisdom had not, thus far, misled him. He suited Grace admirably, and she suited him. All that was lacking was the spark on his side. In every other sense he loved her. If affection can be called love.

David, his troubled face glowing in the firelight, leant forward and again dug the poker between the iron bars. If only Lucy Rennie hadn't crossed his path; hadn't lit that spark that Grace, with all her love for him,

195

had so far failed to light. The thought of Lucy troubled him. She roused the male in him. Her womanhood was coming, more and more, to obsess his mind; to open up for him a vista of enchantment, the primitive enchantment of holding in his arms the woman who could arouse this fever within him. For the moment he could not bother to determine if the feelings she had awakened were good or bad. At least they were natural. The fact of Lucy Rennie clouded his judgment.

David, a man of thirty-one, belonged to a time, and a people who, however unfanatical their own beliefs, had inherited a strict background of behaviour, where irregularity was abhorred. In other words, David's education as a male of the human species was almost non-existent. And the lack of it now, in his dilemma, was causing him cruel distress.

Although he could not see clearly, this young man belonged to an honourable world. His mind was constantly on Lucy Rennie. At the same time he found himself caught up in self-loathing at his disloyalty to Grace. There was no peace, no rest for him anywhere. How could he go on with his engagement in the present state of his feelings? And yet how could he break it? Could he throw all the kindness of Robert Dermott and his wife back into their faces? And Grace? Was he to take her great tenderness towards him (he knew it now for what it was) and throw this, too, back at her?

As he sat moodily stabbing his fire, he remembered the solemn promise he had made himself on that morning he had asked Grace to marry him: the promise to stand by her and see the thing through. But would it be right to go on? He could not even decide what was the honourable course. David got up and paced his room.

And even if he were free, what of Lucy Rennie? Had she any interest in him? He could not tell. His infatuation encouraged him to think she was not indifferent. But he had not seen enough of her. She had been friendly and charming to him. That was all. The image of her stood before him. Her elegant person. The faint perfume she used. The moving quality of her voice. Her quick, easy gaiety. Her pleasant good manners.

This room was intolerable. He would go across and wish Bel and Arthur a good New Year.

II

As David was being led upstairs by Bel's parlourmaid Sarah he heard a hum of talk.

'Are they alone, Sarah? Who's with them?'

'Baillie and Mrs. McNairn, Mr. David.'

If David could have turned and run, he

197

would have done so. But Sarah would have thought him crazy.

As she opened the door to announce him, he was met by the noise of family voices – what, in a blither moment, he would have called the Moorhouse roar. They all seemed to be speaking at once, and all speaking loud.

The first voice to succeed in disengaging itself from the general din was the baillie's. Possibly because he was used to shouting.

'Hullo! hullo! Here's the shipowner himself! A good New Year to you!' George, dazzled by the eminence to which David was rising, advanced to greet him cordially.

David bade everybody a Happy New Year. He kissed Bel and his sisters, Phœbe and Mary, and shook hands with Arthur and George. After all perhaps the family wasn't so bad. There's something about finding oneself among them; even if, in happier, less care-burdened times, they all seemed utterly commonplace.

'Phœbe says you all had a splendid time at Duntrafford!' George McNairn went on. Phœbe, on being asked, had merely told him that her stay at Duntrafford had been 'quite nice'. But the baillie's mind liked to dwell on magnificence.

Like Phœbe, David echoed that it had been 'quite nice'.

'And what about Dermott Ships Limited?

They haven't made you chairman yet?' George went on facetiously.

There was nothing for David to do but allow George's gloatings over his good fortune to exhaust themselves – the good fortune that was weighing so heavily on his spirit.

George having finished, Bel was waiting to speak. 'I'm very glad to see you,' she said, 'because I got a letter from Lucy Rennie today. It's about the concert here. She writes that she is willing to sing, but she must be back in London by the middle of next week. She has engagements there. She suggests Saturday afternoon of this week. It's giving us a very short time. That's why I've asked George and Mary here tonight, to try to get people together quickly.'

The mere name of Lucy Rennie had thrown David's senses into confusion. He was glad that the baillie was pacing the room importantly, repeating, in what he thought was a voice loaded with modesty, that surely he, with his little bit of influence, could find one or two people who weren't nobody.

'We want Grace and her mother to come. And perhaps they could suggest some people who would care to hear Miss Rennie.' It was Bel's secret hope that the Dermotts' friends would, for smartness's sake, outnumber the friends of the McNairns.

David promised to do what he could.

What else was there to do? The foundations of his existence might be rocking, but the bright pattern of the surface must, in the meantime, continue unbroken.

Bel now called upon Mary and David to discuss the arrangements for Miss Rennie's afternoon. That is, Bel did the talking while Mary, determined to do as little as possible, sat applauding every proposal that would bring no exertion to herself, and constantly looking round to see if Sarah were bringing tea. David merely sat and gave a dazed assent.

'Well, that's all that settled,' Bel ended gaily. 'Now the next step is to let Miss Rennie know what we intend to do, and make sure that it suits her. Could you run up and see her, David? You don't mind, do you? Perhaps at lunchtime tomorrow? It has to be at once.'

No. David would be glad to do anything to help. The pattern was unwinding itself. He could not stop it. And he could not hide from himself that he was pleased to have this excuse for going to Lucy Rennie again. Next week she would be gone out of his reach – unless?

'Here you are, then, David. Here's a short note to Miss Rennie. Oh, here's Sarah with tea. Mary dear, you'll wait and have some tea, won't you?'

Mary, who was making no move, thanked

Bel and stayed where she was. 'Just when you are at your desk, Bel dear, could you write me the recipe for your chocolate cake? I see Sarah's brought one up. You've always been going to do it.'

But Bel, remembering some other, urgent point about the concert, was in sudden deep talk with David. Phœbe poured out tea, and Mary was foiled again.

III

Lucy Rennie's morning had been busy with pupils, and she was grateful, having finished lunch, to take a cup of coffee to an easy chair by the fire. Outside it was very cold and a little foggy. A letter received this morning had told her it was mild in London. She was glad to be going back.

But it was not only the weather that made Lucy glad to leave Glasgow. It was time she was gone. In London she had found her niche. That was her world. It was a friendly, easy world, with its own standards. And, if you were tactful, were not infirm of purpose, and were a hard-working artist – all of which attributes Lucy, having long since shed illusion, had acquired, you could make a very good life of it. London was her home now. It was there that she could breathe.

She had been glad to leave Greenhead

yesterday. She, her father and her sister had made good-natured attempts to reach each other. But Lucy's life had thrust them too far apart. Her ways of thought, the education she had picked up, had set up too many barriers. She was better, really, not to see them very much. The thought distressed her a little. It was dreary to face the truth that the bonds between herself and her relatives had fallen away.

But that was not all the reason for her disquietude. There was David Moorhouse. When she had seen him at Duntrafford she had become aware that he was attracted to herself.

Lucy bent over the fire, thinking. It wouldn't do. She had no intention of starting up a flirtation with David. If it had been someone of her own world, who knew the rules of the game – but with a man of the Moorhouse world, the world she had broken from... No. Besides, David Moorhouse had always been the little boy of her memory, a part of the picture of her not unpleasant childhood. There had been one or two close friendships with men, since she had grown up. But David would always hold a unique place. He had grown into a handsome man, in no way belying the promise of his boyhood. But she did not want to know this man. Much better to leave as undisturbed as might be the picture of the boy – to leave the grown man to the young woman he had chosen, and go her own ways in peace.

The door was thrown open and the man she was thinking of stood before her.

'David! How are you? Come in. What has brought you at this time of day?'

'It's about Bel's concert, Lucy. I can't stay.'

'You look cold. Take off your overcoat for five minutes, and I'll give you a cup of coffee.'

He did as he was told. 'Well, only for a minute. I've gone into a new business, you know: Grace's father is taking me into partnership.'

'I know. I heard all about it. Some people have all the luck.'

'Have they?'

'Well, aren't you having luck, David? I would call you very ungrateful if you said you weren't.'

'Yes, I dare say I am lucky.'

But the brightness of David's prospects proved but a flat topic between them. So Lucy took Bel's letter, read it, and discussed its contents with him.

'Well, I think that's about everything.' Lucy's contribution to the concert arrangements had not taken long. And now that she came to think of it, she had done all the talking. She expected David to go now, but he stayed on, making disjointed remarks, unable, it would seem, to take himself away.

He asked her what she did in London; how she lived. She gave him suitable answers. There was something very innocent about all this; dangerously naïve. If she had disliked David it would have been easy to show him the door. Young men at this emotional pitch were not unknown to her, and in the past she had dealt with them clear-headedly, as it had suited her. But she couldn't do it with David. He was too much a part of memory. And she was beginning to feel that if she were not careful, her own emotions would be caught.

She stood up. 'David,' she said, 'I'm sorry to have to send you away. But I must go out soon.'

He stood up, too, as it seemed to her, reluctantly. For a moment they were together on the hearthrug. Quickly, Lucy moved away and ran one finger over the keys of her piano as though she were impatient to practise.

'Lucy, can I ask a favour?'

She turned and faced him.

'Will you sing the song you played and sang at Duntrafford? You know, the one you said you would sing at Bel's concert.'

No. She wasn't going to help him to an emotional scene. She allowed a smile to spread over her face, and permitted herself a little burst of laughter. 'What a sentimental old thing you are, David! YOU want me to sing that song to you, just because that girl of yours liked it.'

'No, Lucy, I–'

'Here's your coat, David! I'll sing it for you all on Saturday. She'll be there, won't she?' She held up David's coat for him to get into.

There was nothing left for him to do but to put it on, say goodbye and go. His face, as he went, had the same embarrassed expression as when, in childhood, they had been caught together at the same forbidden prank and he was being roundly scolded.

She laughed as she went to her window and watched him as his muffled figure receded down the hill. But there was wistfulness and self-distrust in her laughter.

Chapter Sixteen

Grace was quickly becoming part of the family. Bel sat looking at her with approval over a cup of eleven o'clock tea. Only a day had elapsed since Bel had decided to have Miss Rennie's concert on Saturday afternoon, and here was Grace up to Grosvenor Terrace this morning already.

Yesterday David had sent her a note by her father. She had come to find in what direction she could be helpful. A strong sympathy was growing up between Bel and Grace

Dermott. They were both well-intentioned women, though Bel's goodness suffered, at times, from a thick overlay of snobbery and petty scheming. Grace was simpler, and had none of that unimaginative unattractive shrewdness, which many comfortable Lowland Scots mistake for common sense. But she had some of her parents' organising instinct, and she was putting this at Bel's service this morning.

She sat at the table in the back parlour, pencil in hand, making suggestions and writing down one item after the other. A carpenter to unscrew hinges. The florist. The caterer. She would make inquiries of all sorts, and come back to tell Bel.

Grace's mother, Bel learnt, had a list of people to whom she was writing at once, telling them that they must attend Mrs. Arthur Moorhouse's concert and give liberally for the distress in the city. Bel knew Mrs. Robert Dermott well enough to know that these people would regard her letters as royal commands and come, unless their excuses for staying away were very solid. Mrs. Dermott's list was large and contained many important names in the West of Glasgow. It would all be very gratifying to look back upon. But the thought of these august people at Grosvenor Terrace, and how they should be treated, fussed Bel. Grace must stand beside her, tell her who was who, and see her through. They were, of course, the people Bel wanted in her house. Much more so than the McNairns' honest City fathers and their wives, who would do well enough if she could do no better. She caught herself wondering if she dare send a note to Mary saying that, very unfortunately, Mrs. Robert Dermott had been over-zealous and had already invited as many people as the room would hold; and would Mary and George please delay inviting anyone until Bel saw how numbers were going. But even Bel's nerve failed her before this culminating snobbery. She must take her chance with Mary's guests.

Everything, then, was satisfactorily arranged, and Bel was settling down with Grace to a final cup of tea when Sophia opened the parlour door and walked in.

'Hullo, dear. How are you? And Grace? This is nice! How are you both? A Happy New Year. I had such a nice bedside book from your mother, Bel, for Christmas. I must write and thank her. I haven't had time yet. *From a Thinker's Garden* it was called. You know. Nice, quiet, wee bits from great writers, just to make you think about life. Splendid to read just before you go to sleep.'

Had Bel not been so full of arrangements, and so resentful of Sophia's intrusion, the picture of her fussy sister-in-law in bed beside her speechless bear of a husband, reading nice, quiet, wee bits and thinking about life, would have made it hard to keep solemn. Especially if David had been there to wink behind Sophia's back. But this morning there was too much to be thought about.

'*Could* I have a cup of tea, dear?' Sophia went on.

With the best grace Bel could muster, she pulled the bell-pull by the fire.

The spate of talk continued: 'I was out shopping, and I suddenly had a terrible hunger to see some flowers. I get it sometimes in winter. So I went into the Botanic Gardens and walked through the glass-houses. The bulbs are really lovely, dear. You should go. And just as I came out, I looked across here. I could see your house from up there quite clearly. Wasn't it funny? It's because there are no leaves on the trees. And I saw Sarah out at the door. She was polishing the bell and the letterbox. And I thought: "I'll hurry across and walk straight in, and give Bel a surprise!"'

A third cup arrived at this moment, and Bel succeeded in producing something that looked like a wan smile of invitation as she poured out tea. Sensing danger ahead, she would fain have warned Grace to say nothing of the concert arrangements. But before she knew where she was, Grace had innocently told Sophia of Saturday's doings. The inevitable happened.

'My dears! How interesting! I must tell dozens of people to come! And to think, Bel, that it was through me that you met Lucy Rennie! You remember, on the bridge?'

No; Bel had not remembered that it was through Sophia that she had met Lucy Rennie, and this, having now been pointed out to her, was an inconvenient fact that she could neither deny nor dismiss from her conscience. But with Sophia, what was to be done?

Sophia went on: 'You see, I know a lot of nice church people, who would be terribly interested about Lucy, and probably have nothing else to do on Saturday afternoon. I dare say they would be glad to give a sixpence or two; especially if there was a cup of tea.'

It was some support to Bel to see that even Grace's guilelessness was worried by the implications of Sophia's offer. Like herself, Grace had no doubt been thinking, not in sixpences, but in five-pound notes. She must rally her forces. As a preliminary, she invited Sophia to have a piece of the chocolate cake of Mary's coveting.

'It's very kind of you, Sophia,' she said, assuming what she hoped looked like a grateful expression, 'but I have just been worrying about numbers a little, dear. You see, George McNairn is asking some of the baillies and their wives, because it's a town charity. And Grace's mother has been very kind and written several people she thinks might give us handsome donations. So if you wouldn't mind waiting until I let you know – I am so afraid of not having room for everybody. You'll come yourself with William, of course, won't you, dear?'

'Oh, of course. I quite see.' Sophia's face fell. She had hoped to repay some casual entertainment not in her own house, but in Bel's. 'But you *will* let me know if there is room?'

Like the queen of mendacity she could be, Bel assured Sophia that she would.

II

Presently, and much to Bel's relief, Sophia rose to go. She explained at length that she still had shopping to do, and must be home to see to the children's midday meal. Bel's bad conscience prompted her to kiss Sophia affectionately, and see her with more than usual attention to the door. She opened it with a parting word of guilty endearment, to find Miss Rennie standing on the step outside in the act of ringing the bell that Sarah had so lately polished.

'Lucy! How nice to see you! I'm coming to hear you sing on Saturday! How are you?' Sophia burst out.

Miss Rennie had a bright purposeful smile

for both the ladies, and bade them good morning.

For a moment Sophia lingered on the doorstep. It was obvious to Bel that she was considering whether she ought to come back into the house and have a friendly talk with Lucy. But that would be altogether too maddening; when there was so much to arrange; when Grace was there to help with her counsel; and when Miss Rennie had come with the expressed intention of talking business. Bel was well aware that a flicker of an eyelid would have brought Sophia back inside. But guilty conscience or no guilty conscience, her eyelid did not flicker. So there was nothing left for Sophia to do but go down the front doorsteps to the pavement, while Bel's door was closed behind her.

'See who's here,' Bel called to Grace as she led Lucy into the parlour and rang for yet more tea. Bel was delighted. She had not expected Lucy; at all events not so soon as this morning. Now they could really push on with arrangements.

Lucy greeted Grace with politeness, trusted she had had a pleasant journey from Ayrshire, and expressed her own opinions as to how pleasant the meetings with old and new friends at Duntrafford had been. 'David came to see me yesterday,' she went on. 'He brought me your letter, Mrs. Moorhouse. And I thought I had better come up to see

you as soon as I could to tell you my arrangements and hear what you were doing.' Lucy
accepted a seat and suggested her programme. They then went upstairs, where
Lucy ran her fingers over the piano, was tactfully doubtful if it was just the most suitable
piano for her accompanist, who would also
play pieces, and received Bel's immediate
permission to choose a hired piano and have
it sent out from town at once.

Grace had come with them. Bel kept trying to draw her into the discussion. She had
been so helpful already this morning. But,
somehow, the light had gone out of her. Bel
caught herself wondering if, after all, Grace
were moody and spoilt. It might be. Though
she had shown no sign of it before. As they
descended the stairs again, Grace said she
must go. She would see to the things she
had undertaken to do this morning, and
would call back later to let Bel know. Bel did
not keep her. But she wondered.

'What a charming girl Miss Dermott is,'
Lucy Rennie was saying as she came back
into the parlour.

'Yes. We think David's very lucky,' Bel
answered, heartlessly enough.

'Miss Dermott's very lucky, too, Mrs.
Moorhouse. You see, I know David quite
well. We were great friends as children. It's
been quite a – what shall I say? – bit of the
past for me to see him again.'

212

'And what do you think of him now?'

'I've always thought David was a darling.'

Bel flinched a little at a young woman calling a young man a 'darling'. Miss Rennie had picked up this unScottish expression in London, she supposed.

'I shall always be fond of David,' Lucy went on. 'I'm glad he's marrying someone nice.'

It would have taken someone much less alert, much less sensitive to overtones than Bel, to miss linking Grace's sudden departure with what Lucy said. Had something happened at Duntrafford? Had David's behaviour to Lucy given Grace cause to be jealous? Or had the mere fact that Lucy claimed the freedom of an old friendship thrown a spoilt only daughter out of temper? But instinctively Bel sided with Grace. Grace was one of the tribe now. This woman was, after all, just a singer – a Bohemian outsider. The Moorhouse family, in addition to David himself, had much to gain from David's marriage to a Dermott. She must give Miss Rennie a tactful warning.

Bel smiled pleasantly. 'Yes,' she said, 'I think I can say David's a special friend of mine, too. You see, he was just a boy when he came to Glasgow. In some ways I took the place of his mother. He tells me most things. I know Grace Dermott is everything to him now.' She looked steadily into Lucy's eyes.

213

'The Dermotts are very rich people, I hear,' Lucy said solemnly.

Bel fell into Lucy's trap. 'Very. It's a splendid connection. Dermott Ships, of course. David is to be made a partner.'

'So he'll be among the great and the mighty. Some people have everything thrown at them, don't they, Mrs. Moorhouse?' Lucy smiled, looking steadily back at Bel for a moment. Then with a little laugh she added: 'While people like myself have to fight for everything.' After a moment's pause, and as Bel made no reply, she went on: 'Now, you were asking about the tuning of the piano. Well, you see—'

Bel felt, somehow, that it was she who had received the warning, as Lucy, serene and sure of herself, went on with the arrangements that had brought her to Grosvenor Terrace.

III

Bel's concert was arranged for three o'clock on Saturday afternoon. Grace and her mother arrived at two, Grace having promised to see Bel through the final stages of preparation. And as there was nowhere else convenient for her mother to be, she had to bring Mrs. Dermott with her. Grace's mother was an awkward person to have in the house at such a time. She came in, giving loud instructions that no one was to mind her. But the great Mrs. Robert Dermott was the sort of person one had to mind. Her presence filled every house she entered.

Bel's children, Arthur, Isabel and Tom, were gathered together, a rather forlorn little group, in the hall, waiting for their Aunt Mary's nursemaid to call for them and take them to spend the afternoon with their McNairn cousins at Albany Place. Mrs. Dermott demanded of the harassed mother to be introduced to them, asked them their names, and bestowed half-crowns upon them. All of which wasted precious time. For Bel had to make sure that they were being polite, and answering their new Aunt Grace's mother nicely, while caterers were coming in with trays of cakes and drums of ice-cream, and every other kind of trades-man was coming to the front door instead of going properly to the back, and all sorts of last-minute activity were under way.

Having at last finished with the children, and still shouting to everyone not to mind her in the least, Mrs. Dermott said she would just go upstairs and sit quietly in the drawing-room. But Bel had continually to go out and in to see to this, that and the other. And, each time, Mrs. Dermott waylaid her with observations that she had to stop, listen to, and reply to.

'Do you think it's wise, Mrs. Moorhouse, to have the piano so near that window?'

'I do think your flowers look nice. Grace said she was giving you some from our greenhouses. Now, which are they?'

'By the way, Mrs. Moorhouse, do you know if Lady McCulloch is coming this afternoon? I wonder if I remembered to write to her?'

'I do think these are nice town houses. It's not so very long since they were built. Now, will it be as much as twenty years ago?'

Really, dates at this moment! But Mrs. Dermott was so accustomed to making her presence felt, that merely to sit on a chair in an empty room trying to reverse the process was almost killing her.

How much better it would have been had she sent a cheque and good wishes, as Margaret Ruanthorpe-Moorhouse had done.

At half-past two Sophia arrived with her husband. She was nursing a grievance. Bel had made no move about the church people Sophia had wanted to invite. Bel, however, was long past noticing Sophia's grievances. Without telling them that Mrs. Dermott was sitting solitary and ready to pounce, she directed them to the drawing-room, and heard Mrs. Dermott exclaim: 'Ah, Mrs. Butter! There you are!' before the door closed. When, some minutes later, necessity forced Bel to look in, Mrs. Dermott and

216

Sophia were enjoying themselves hugely, shouting across William, who sat between them, his fat hands clasped before him on his comfortable stomach, saying nothing.

But now people were really beginning to arrive. Maids were sent to their proper stations, and Bel and Arthur, with Grace to help them with names, had taken up their places in the drawing-room. Bel had every reason to be pleased that Mrs. Dermott had shown interest. Everybody who was anybody, or at any rate the females of the breed, were filing into her drawing-room. After today, Bel felt certain, the Arthur Moorhouses would be somebodies in Kelvinside. And she was glad to see the one or two town dignitaries whom the McNairns had sent. Official Glasgow was there, in addition to fashionable Glasgow.

At ten minutes to three the McNairns themselves arrived. They came upstairs, and standing for a moment breathless on the landing, hoped to make a pompous entry. But the room was so full of the highly important, that nobody took any notice of them. Perhaps it was annoyance at this that caused Mary to turn to Bel and express the hope that Miss Rennie and her accompanist had arrived safely. Bel sent Phœbe to see. No, Miss Rennie was not yet there. Had she got lost? For some moments Bel was thrown into a panic. She turned to her husband,

'Arthur, Lucy Rennie's not here! Surely she should be here by now!'

At an easier moment for her, Arthur would have teased his wife. But now, standing close alongside of her, he pressed the hand that was near his own saying: 'It's all right, Bel. The lassie knows the time.'

And presently, as the grandfather clock on the stair was preparing to strike three, David appeared from downstairs to say that Lucy had arrived with her accompanist, and that they would be ready to begin almost directly.

IV

David, conscious now of his feelings towards Lucy, had come unwillingly this afternoon. He was filled with apprehension, almost fear. Things had passed beyond his control. And he was afraid that, in some way, he might show it. Very quickly now he must make up his mind what must be done. But today, of all days, that surface pattern must still remain unbroken.

When he came to look back, this afternoon took on a nightmare unreality. Bel's packed drawing-room. The pots of greenhouse plants. The heavy scent of Roman hyacinths. The black, shining grand piano, brought in, not to be a decoration in a rich man's house, but as an instrument for hands that could use it. Stray, tormenting details that were to build up memory. Now, as he listened to Lucy's singing, he felt the full force of her. Her disciplined performance. Her self-assurance, that, for him at least, had a certain gallant appeal. Her obvious accomplishment. Her ability to please. And above all her womanliness. There was nothing, it seemed, of the essential Lucy frittered away. All of her seemed to be brought to bear. He no more understood the source of Lucy Rennie's power than he had understood the power of the great actor he had seen as 'Hamlet' in the autumn. David was troubled, dazed, conscience-stricken and enchanted.

At an interval in her recital she spoke to him as she moved from the room. 'Well, David, I sang your song for you.'

'Did you?' He was too stupid to dissemble.

'Oh, David! I sang it with the other Schumann songs. Didn't you recognise it?' She passed on with a laugh.

'David dear, come here.' It was Mrs. Dermott's loud voice. 'Lady McCulloch, I want you to meet my son-in-law, at least, nearly my son-in-law, David Moorhouse. Grace and he are being married at the beginning of March.'

It was as though he were acting in a terrible charade, going through movements that were merely mechanical.

But presently the other players would be gone, and Grace, Lucy and himself would have to play out this distressing game to its unrelenting finish.

Chapter Seventeen

Bel sat combing her long fair hair in front of her mirror. Arthur bent over her, tying his white tie. This Sunday morning it was his turn to stand by the plate in the Ramshorn Church. The reflection of his narrow, handsome face, with its high cheekbones, his black hair and his trim side-whiskers, was the reflection of decorum itself.

'Are ye coming to the Kirk this morning, my dear?' he asked, giving the bow of his tie a final tug.

'Of course.'

'I thought maybe ye would be tired.'

'No, I'm all right.' Bel was surprised. Normally there was never any question as to who should go to church and who shouldn't. Arthur's question implied that yesterday's concert had exhausted her. Which was quite the reverse of true. Bel was living in the exhilaration of a real success. The sum she had raised for the distressed children of the city was far beyond what she had expected.

And, more important perhaps, she felt she had made a social hit. The fact that certain prominent people had been in her house and had contributed generously did not put her on calling terms with them. But it had made them aware of her existence.

Arthur was pleased with her. She had grasped this from the tone of his voice. He was even prepared to spare her the discipline of Sunday morning worship, a thing almost unheard of in his orthodox Scottish family. But Bel wanted to appear in church. Sophia and Mary would be there for her to queen over. And her mother, old Mrs. Barrowfield, who had declined to come to the concert and mix with grand folks, would be there too, and would have greedy ears for Bel's success.

Bel and Arthur finished dressing, and prepared to go downstairs to their Sunday ham and eggs. As they passed the drawing-room, there was the noise of children's voices. All their three children were jumping about among the rows of caterer's chairs, arranging themselves in the jungle among the welter of flowers and decorative plants, and even daring to touch the notes on the great, strange piano. Arthur commanded them sternly to remember it was the Sabbath Day, and to come to breakfast.

All this morning Bel was floating on air. Her feelings were somewhat those of a young prima donna who, after years of preparation, has made a triumphant debut. There was a wintry sunshine this morning as she, her husband, Phœbe and little Arthur set out on the long journey to church in Ingram Street. As the cab-horse jogged down through Hillhead towards town, she felt like royalty, as though almost it was incumbent upon her to bow her fair and fashionable head from the window, as she went by.

At the church door her mother met her with a 'Dear me, Bel, what are ye all dressed up for?'

'Dressed up, Mother? What do you mean?'

'Ye know fine what I mean. How did ye get on yesterday?'

'Bel's concert was a great success, Mrs. Barrowfield,' Arthur replied, preparing to take up his station by the plate.

His wife herded her mother along with the others into the family pew, smiling the while with regal affection. Having got them all seated, and seen them supplied with hymn-books and Bibles, she raised her veil and, inclining her head to her beautifully gloved hands, said her prayers with great elegance. The sermon, as it happened, turned out to be on the subject of Christian charity – a subject which did nothing to lower Bel's self-esteem.

Everyone, it seemed, approved of her this morning. After the service, Sophia, forgetting her own grievance, did her best to

222

envelop her in the usual flood of talk. Two baillies' wives who had actually been at Grosvenor Terrace yesterday, and had been so much impressed by the augustness of Bel's audience that they had given more than they had meant to, pressed forward to congratulate her. Mary, finding herself included in the aura of Bel's glory, decided to bask in it for the time and to leave some criticism she had been incubating until later.

It was no wonder that Arthur seemed pleased, Bel reflected as, just back from church, she sat once more at the mirror straightening her hair before she went down to the Sunday dinner.

Again she saw the reflection of her husband behind her. 'Well, dear?' she said pleasantly, continuing with her toilet.

Arthur sat down on a chair near her. 'Something has just come into my head, Bel,' he began.

Bel cast him a fleeting smile of encouragement.

'I was just thinking that maybe it was time ye had a carriage and pair of your own.'

Bel's heart gave a bound. Arthur had done more for her than he knew. He, the husband of her love, was giving full and final approval. Had she obeyed her impulses, she would have jumped up and thrown her arms about his neck. But she had known him too long to do anything so emotional. It would merely embarrass him. A little resistance, indeed, would fix his purpose more surely, and confirm his opinion of her careful good sense. She turned to him, her comb in her hand, and said: 'Oh, Arthur! But in these times? Can we afford one?'

Arthur sat considering. His wife let him take his time.

'Well,' he said at last, 'ye see, David's not taking money out of the business now, and the papers say things will be better by the summer. And what with you getting to be such a swell and everything.'

That was too much for Bel. She got up, told him he was an old silly, kissed him and sat down again.

'But what about the coach-house?' she said presently, 'and the McCrimmons?'

'They're decent folks,' Arthur said, pondering.

'Surely we could get McCrimmon some work, Arthur. Phœbe says he's getting an artificial foot.'

'How can we put the McCrimmons out, my dear?'

'It's not a case of putting them out, Arthur. It's a case of letting McCrimmon himself know that we thought it was time he was looking about him.'

'There's not much work to be had,' Arthur said doubtfully, adding as a rueful afterthought: 'And for a lame man—'

'No. But, after all, we're not turning them into the street. We can wait until he finds something. It's a question of giving him notice. That's all.'

'I wouldna like to do that, Bel.'

'That's nonsense, dear. I'm going in to-morrow morning to pay Mrs. McCrimmon for helping in the kitchen during the concert yesterday. I'll tell them.'

'Very well.' Arthur gave a wan assent. He saw again the quarters from which he had rescued these people. He wished, now, that he had never, in a sudden burst of admiration for his wife, said the word carriage to her. She was doing very well as she was.

II

Bel's aspirations had put her on the rack. If her feet, this morning, had trodden clouds of realised hopes, this afternoon they were weighted with lead. But her purpose held. She would tell McCrimmon first thing in the morning that, whenever he was well enough, he must find employment and take his family elsewhere.

She spent the rest of the day wrestling with her feelings.

Common sense was, as it so often is, on the side of ambition. It was ridiculous, she

225

assured herself, that there should be any difficulty about these people going. She had shown them every kindness. Most of the actual attention had been paid to them by Phœbe, but that was because the girl had less to do than she, Bel, had; and had a mania for lame ducks anyway. But she had refused none of Phœbe's requests for them. The little McCrimmon children had been clad in the cast-off clothing of her own children. She had invented work for the woman to do, so that her stiff, Highland pride should not feel, too sharply, the sting of charity. She had, more than once, committed herself to the laudable fraud of ordering larger amounts of meat than she knew her own household could need, so that the remainder should be taken to the coach-house by Phœbe with the request that the McCrimmons might be so good as to eat it, and thus save waste.

No, Bel assured herself, she had nothing to be ashamed of in her treatment of them. But her first duty was to her husband and her children. Arthur had come out West because he wanted to keep up 'a certain position'. And very rightly. That he was able to do so was the reward of his industry. And a carriage was part of the paraphernalia this 'certain position' demanded. She, herself, was doing what she could for him. Yesterday she had filled his house with the right people – people among whose children she looked, when the time came, to marry her own. Surely the first thing to be done was to live as these people lived.

Thus, for the remainder of this outwardly uneventful Sunday, did Bel struggle with her softer self. She did not dare to discuss the matter further with her husband, and still less with his sister.

Before breakfast on Monday morning she took her purse in her hand, and set forth to carry out her intentions. The earlier the better. There were, after all, times when feelings must be set aside and duty done as impersonally as might be.

The little stone staircase leading up to the McCrimmons' living-quarters was, Bel noted, scrubbed clean and decorated with ripples of pipeclay. There was the piping of children's voices. She knocked. On the other side of the door there was a sudden hush, then footsteps. Bel, as she stood waiting, became aware of her own heart-beats. It was not the ascent of the short stairs that had brought them to her consciousness. As the door was opened by Mrs. McCrimmon, Bel fixed a smile on her face and summoned her resolve. The woman fell back respectfully at the sight of her.

'Good morning Mrs. McCrimmon. I hope I'm not disturbing you too early in the morning, but I have a lot to do today, after Saturday.'

'I could be coming across and helping, Mam.'

'Oh, no, thanks. The men will be taking away things. But there's nothing the maids can't do by themselves.'

The woman made no direct reply to this, but asked Bel to step inside.

Bel looked about her in the bare kitchen. The family were at breakfast. The two little children, in mended clothes only too familiar to her, and their father, in a cast-off suit of Arthur's, were sitting over bowls of porridge. There was nothing else on the scrubbed table but that and mugs of milk for the children. It looked a dull enough meal to Bel, but at least it was filling. The room was warm. Arthur had seen to that. And it was clean. It was furnished with the McCrimmons' few shabby things and some old furniture Phœbe had borrowed. A discarded nursery rug lay in front of the fire. The man withdrew his footless leg from the stool that supported it, and made to stand up in Bel's presence.

'No. Please sit down.' But he stood, balancing on one foot, and holding the table. Bel asked how his leg did and when he would be able to wear an artificial foot. She asked for the children, and tried to make them tell her their names. If there had been more to ask she would have asked it, for now she was struggling with her resolution. She opened her purse.

'I just came across to pay you what I owe you for helping on Saturday, Mrs. McCrimmon.' She took the money out, laid it on the table, and smiled at the stiff woman beside her. She was surprised to see that McCrimmon's wife had gone red to the roots of her hair, and that there were tears in her eyes.

'I should not be taking this, Mam. You've done a lot for us.'

'Nonsense, Mrs. McCrimmon. We can't expect you to work for nothing.' Bel stopped. There was nothing now to say, except to tell these people they must leave their place of refuge at the earliest possible moment, so that she, Bel Moorhouse, could install a properly trained and fashionable coachman.

As she stood, hesitating and embarrassed, the two Highlanders looking at her could have no idea of the battle that raged in the heart of this handsome, City lady. It was not the first time that snobbery had assailed Bel's tenderness. And yet, it is perfect truth to say that Bel despised herself for what she next found herself saying.

'McCrimmon, Mr. Moorhouse has decided to have a carriage.' She stopped for a moment, but the cloud of apprehension that crossed their faces made her hurry on. 'And we were wondering if, when you get your artificial foot, you would like to be our coachman?'

As she crossed the back garden on the way to the house she chid her cowardice for having tied a Highlander, unstylish, uncouth and lame, about her neck, but her step was light, and a weight was lifted from her.

She found her husband alone in the breakfast-room. 'I'm afraid I've asked Mc-Crimmon to be the coachman, Arthur,' she said, flushing guiltily.

Arthur smiled with offensive complacency. 'That's fine, my dear. It's just what I expected,' was all he said, and stirred his tea with what Bel considered was a ridiculously unfashionable vigour.

III

Mrs. Dermott and Grace had taken David back to Aucheneame. He was bewildered and exhausted. He had not wanted to come with them after the concert, but, until he had decided what he must do, there was no excuse for absenting himself. As he sat in the carriage opposite Grace, he noticed that she, too, seemed tired and out of spirits. This was not perhaps surprising. At Grosvenor Terrace she had been running here, there and everywhere.

Neither of them spoke much. Nor were they required to. Mrs. Dermott, stimulated as she was by any gathering of people, talked without ceasing.

'I do think the whole thing was excellently arranged, David. Mrs. Arthur Moorhouse must be a born organiser. I really must ask her to join us on the Indigent Mothers. There's a vacancy on the committee.'

'What a beautiful singer Miss Rennie is! She reminds me more of Trebelli-Bettini than anybody. You remember we heard her in London, Grace?'

'I like your sister Sophia so much, David. She seems to me so sincere. Her husband doesn't say very much, does he?'

'Lady McCulloch was asking where you were going for your honeymoon. I said I hadn't the faintest idea. I didn't tell her I had strongly advised you to go to Paris. I didn't see any reason to pander to her inquisitiveness.'

David was thankful that the chatter in the carriage went on. And he was thankful, too, that the weekend was filled with the same sort of thing. It was the first weekend since he had entered Dermott Ships, and Robert Dermott was forever making excuses to take him aside and talk business. It was unpleasant for David to go on feeling an impostor. But anything was better than being left alone with Grace. It was easier and less contemptible to be acting a part to her father, than to be acting a part to herself.

But he dreaded the hour or two after the

Sunday midday dinner, for it was then, usually, in the quiet of the afternoon, that he was left alone with her. Even that, however, he managed to avoid. For after their meal, Robert Dermott was seized with feelings of faintness, and David, having with the aid of a manservant helped him to his room, undertook to go with a groom in Mrs. Dermott's pony-trap to seek out and bring back the local doctor. The process of finding him, bringing him, and hearing his pronouncement, that Mr. Dermott was merely suffering from some slight indisposition such as came to men at his time of life, and that he must remember his age and be careful, filled up the hours till tea-time. And beyond even that, indeed, for Mrs. Dermott kept the doctor to tea, and spent a considerable time, now that her anxiety for her husband was allayed, telling him in detail of an attack of pneumatic fever she had had some years ago, how expert his predecessor had been in effecting her cure, and how sorry the district had been to see the former doctor take up practice elsewhere.

In the late evening David came down from Robert Dermott's room. At the request of the old man, who said he felt well now, but had been counselled to remain at home for some days, David had been sitting, note-book in hand, taking down instructions which he was to carry to the office. He had expected to find Mrs. Dermott with Grace. But Grace sat alone by the fire, a book on her knee.

He went to her, and, as was expected of him, bent down and kissed her. She caught his hand and raised it to her lips. He stood, his back to the fire, fanning out his long coat-tails and looking down upon her. She seemed tired, even a little worn, as she looked up at him.

'Well, Grace?'

'Well, David?'

'Your father's all right. He's been ordering me about as if I was the whole office staff of Dermott Ships put together. You haven't been worrying about him, have you?'

She smiled. 'No, not any more. Although anything like that is very unusual with father. I suppose we must accept that he's getting old.'

David continued warming himself before the fire for some moments, looking in front of him, occupied with his own thoughts.

'David.'

The tone of her voice made him look down quickly. He saw that Grace's colour had risen, that she was trying to say something.

'Grace? Is anything wrong?'

'Sit down, David. I want to say something to you.'

He sat down upon a stool at her feet. 'My

dearest, is anything–?'

'Let me say this quickly – mother may come in. David, I just wanted to say that any time between now and March, if you – well, feel you don't want to go on with our engagement, I want you to know that – that I'm not holding you in any way. I don't want you to feel bound, because–' Her voice stopped, she could say no more.

He rose to his feet and, bending down, kissed her once again. He felt a great tenderness towards her. His sensibilities were tortured by her own. And yet, in the act of reassuring her, he found himself asking what signs she had seen; how she had come to guess? He felt that had he known passion, rather than tenderness towards her, he might have raged; demanding why she wanted to be free of him, why she wanted to ruin his life? But he dare not ask these questions, for the very asking of them would be untruthful.

But Grace seemed comforted by the reassurance he could give her, and when her mother came to them there was no sign that any storm had been.

IV

In the middle of the following morning Bel received a note from David. It was delivered by hand, and read as follows:

'Please meet me in Ferguson and Forester's restaurant in Buchanan Street today at one. We can have a private room. I must talk to you. I am in great trouble. Don't tell anyone that you are meeting me.

'DAVID.'

For Bel, David's request was highly inconvenient. She was setting her house to rights after Saturday's disturbance. But Bel was fond of David. She must go to him somehow.

She called to Phœbe, who was going out: 'Phœbe dear, I wonder if you would mind staying in this morning. The men are coming to take away the grand piano. And some chairs are to go back. And all sorts of other things. Sarah will tell you.'

Phœbe agreed to remain. Although she could not see what she could do to keep the house from damage if the workmen chose to wreck it.

'I've got to go and call on Margaret's doctor.' A white lie never troubled Bel, and this was her best alibi. No one would be so indelicate as to ask questions about Margaret's condition.

Bel was not accustomed to having *tête-à-tête* meals with young men in private rooms of restaurants. She was nothing if not circumspect. The very thought of scandal was abhorrent to her. But every movement and feature of David proclaimed him a Moorhouse, and a brother of her husband. People, if they saw her, might think it unusual, but a midday meal with a brother-in-law could not be accounted fast.

'Well, David? What's all this about?' she said, pulling off her gloves. David, she noted, was looking pale and as though he had not slept.

'We'll order dinner, and then I'll tell you. It was kind of you to come.' He pressed the bell on the wall above their table.

'Did you go to Aucheneame this week-end?' Bel asked conversationally, as they waited.

'Yes.' He told her of Robert Dermott.

'Grace and her mother would be glad to have you.'

'Yes.' His tired eyes did not look at her. They seemed to be glad to fasten themselves on the waiter who presented himself.

When he had gone with his order there was silence.

'Well, David? Tell me.' She felt she must force his confidence. After all, he had brought her here to confide.

'I'm in love with Lucy Rennie, Bel.'

Bel said nothing whatever. She merely sat looking at David, letting the first impact of the words do what they would with her. She must give herself time. Her thoughts turned to Grace Dermott. She liked everything that

Grace stood for. A Moorhouse-Dermott alliance was important to all of them. Yesterday the thought of Lucy Rennie had raised Bel to the seventh heaven. She had allowed her own vanity full scope. But Lucy Rennie was a nobody compared to Grace. Now she could feel nothing but anger and disgust against Lucy. And anger, too, with David for being such a fool. But she must keep her head. For everybody's sake. Not only for David and Grace. Gradually her thoughts began to clear themselves.

Yes, above all, she must keep her head. David would not have told her this unless he had wanted her help. This meant that she had some power with him. She would not dramatise. She would play the whole thing down. She would not fan the flames of his infatuation, either by resisting him or by offering comfort. If she could stifle this, she must do it.

'David,' she said, 'I don't think you *are* in love with Lucy Rennie.'

'Why?'

'Listen, dear. Let me tell you what I think. I dare say you've got – well, a little carried away. You see, Miss Rennie's very nice. But she's the kind of person our family don't know very much about.'

'I've known Lucy Rennie all my life.'

'Not the part of it she spent in London. You see, it's her stock-in-trade to be attractive. I don't say she's doing it consciously with you–'

'How could she? I knew her when she was a child.'

'Perhaps that's made your friendship a little – well, sentimental, David. It's the first time you've met her as a woman. Does she know how you feel?'

'No, not really. But I'm certain she suspects.'

'As far as Miss Rennie's concerned, there may be one or two other young men who are "certain she suspects". Young men think all sorts of things when they're in your state of mind. Especially innocent ones, David.' She saw he did not like this, but she left him to consider for a little, then went on: 'You see, David, this isn't a simple love affair. There's Grace.'

She saw him flinch, as the waiter threw open the door to bring in their soup. The man wondered at this couple sitting so expressionless and silent. He put the plates down and closed the door behind him.

'Grace offered to free me yesterday evening.'

'Grace!' But she must hold on firmly. 'David, have you broken your engagement?'

'No, I hadn't the strength of mind. Remember, her father was ill. You can think how I felt.'

Again Bel considered. 'You love Grace

more than you know.'

'I wish I thought so. I was weak, Bel, that's all.'

'Nonsense, David. I'm glad you didn't. What does Grace know about you and Lucy Rennie?'

'I don't know. She can't know much. There's nothing to know.'

'Was there anything at Duntrafford?'

'No, I don't think so. Except–' He stopped.

'Except what, David?'

'Well, except that we saw Lucy there, more than once.'

'You fell in love with her there, you mean?'

'Perhaps.'

'And do you imagine, David – you of all people – that Grace wouldn't notice?'

He sat thinking, crumbling bread with one hand.

'So that's why she offered to free me,' he said at length. And then, with a look of distress, he muttered: 'Bel, what am I to do?'

Bel sat considering. It would be so easy to plunge into an orgy of womanish emotion with this young man. But if she did, she would merely be indulging herself. And she must remember her own part in this affair. She had, in a sense, encouraged David to engage himself to marry Grace Dermott. She felt some responsibility. And now that she knew Grace, she was sure they were well suited. Both David and Grace were accommodating, easy people. They would do excellently together in the world where they belonged. The pity was that this ridiculous, boyish flare-up hadn't happened when David was twenty-one instead of thirty-one, just when he was on the eve of being more than suitably settled.

As they stood up to go, she gave him her verdict.

'David, don't make any break with Grace yet. I'll think about this, and see you towards the end of the week. At least you owe it to Grace to wait until her father is quite better. It would be very cruel to do anything else. Will you promise?'

'All right, I'll promise.'

As Bel took her way up Buchanan Street, she found herself wondering if a call on Miss Rennie would serve any purpose. But she decided against it. She had had indication already that Lucy would not take her interference. It might, indeed, rouse her resentment and weigh the scales down on the wrong side.

Chapter Eighteen

The mid-January sun was shining in through the large, revealing windows of Aucheneame this morning, finding its way through chilly, starched lace curtains and between hangings of tasselled velvet into spacious, tasteless rooms. It found very little dust in any of them, nor could it catch many dust-particles floating in its own slanting rays, for this house, set on a green hill above the River Clyde, received none of the smoke of industry, and its mistress, competent herself, saw to it that her many servants made diligent use of brush and duster. There was nothing cosy about Aucheneame. Yet on a morning such as this it was not uncheerful, filled with the sunshine as it was, and catching the sun's bright reflection from the winding silver of a river, spotted with the black dots of fussy river craft, steam-tugs and such, as a forest pool is spotted with water-beetles.

But to Grace Dermott it was home, and as she moved about from one bright room to another, doing her Monday-morning household tasks, she was not unhappy.

It would not be true to say that she was quite carefree. But her talk with David last night had lifted most, at least, of the weight that had lain upon her mind since her return from Duntrafford. She was glad she had offered him his freedom. It had been an effort, such as she had never made in her life, but she would not hold him against his will; however much it might cost her.

There was little doubt that David had been attracted by Lucy Rennie. She had some sort of effect upon him that Grace could not understand. She disliked Lucy, but she was not sure that it was fair to blame her. Grace had watched David at Duntrafford. He had flushed and responded to Lucy. He had appeared unnaturally alert when Lucy was present. He had seemed anxious to be in Lucy's company. Above all, the picture of David's face as he sat listening to Lucy's singing on New Year's night had worried and tormented her. It had driven her to a decision. If Lucy's spell seemed still to move David at the concert on Saturday, then, Grace determined, she would offer to let him go.

It had been a terrible step, but she had taken it. And she was glad. It would have been easier for her to be weak; to confide in her mother; to confide, even, in Bel. All kinds of aspects of her problem had jostled each other in her mind, but one decision, at least, had resulted. She would do nothing to coerce David, to drive him into the fold beside her. This was a thing between herself and him, and no one else must interfere. She knew all the Moorhouse family were her friends. She had made them so, anxiously and determinedly. But not from any idea of finding support for herself; merely that she should become as quickly as might be one of themselves as David's wife. Moreover, she had come to realise Bel's position among them. She knew Bel's influence was strong. Bel could easily rouse family feeling on her behalf. Join Moorhouse feeling to the outrage of her parents, and a renegade David would be facing something formidable indeed.

But this was the last thing she wanted for him. She had taken her resolve. Whatever happened between herself and David must have the dignity of secrecy.

Bel's concert, then, had brought things to a head, and Grace had taken her decision. Tremulously jealous, she had watched David, and there had been no mistaking his feelings. Lucy Rennie attracted him. She must offer to let him go.

Grace stood at a window looking out into the winter sunshine. A giant grain-clipper was coming up the river in the tow of what seemed an absurdly small black tug. The bare, spidery rigging showed against the green of the hillside on the far bank. The picture misted a little before her as she smiled to herself.

David had not wanted to be free of her. He

243

had treated her gently, assured her that she was his, and that must be an end of it; that she was worried and overstrung by the illness of her father, and had begun imagining things. She had not argued with him. She could not. And he had reassured her. Or at least, she had allowed herself to be reassured. She had been foolish. That was all. The Lucy Rennie affair must be wholly superficial – something outside of David's control. She must remember Lucy was an old friend of David's, and naturally he must have some affection for her. And she was going back to London this week some time. That would end the matter.

Grace turned to find her mother standing behind her.

'Oh, there you are, Grace,' Mrs. Dermott said. 'I think you might go to your father. He's not feeling very well again this morning. I'm going to send again for the doctor.'

Grace turned and went.

II

Bel's day was to be a disturbed one. She had made straight for home after quitting David. Yet, full as her head was with problems, there was still room for worry about that was happening in Grosvenor Terrace. Was Phœbe seeing to the tradesmen properly? Was her precious house suffering no damage?

The tram-horses puffed their way up into Hillhead and stopped at Botanic Gardens. As Bel alighted and turned into Grosvenor Terrace she was surprised to see a carriage standing in front of her own door. A groom was holding the horses' heads; Sarah was standing on the step looking up and down the Terrace. In a moment more Bel recognised the Dermotts' carriage. What was the matter? Had Grace come to pay a call? But why this unbecoming informality at the door? She hurried her step, and called:

'Sarah, is there anything wrong?'

'It's a message from Mistress Dermott, Mam.'

Bel was now standing by the carriage. 'Good afternoon, MacDonald. I hope there's nothing wrong,' she said, conducting herself, in spite of the confusion of the moment, with what she considered was becoming dignity before Robert Dermott's servants.

'The Master is no' so well, Mam. The Mistress said I was to be giving you this. And be waiting for you.' There was a look of concern in the man's eyes. He handed her an envelope.

'To wait for me?'

'Yes, Mam.'

'I'll read it at once.' She broke the seal where she stood, and read Mrs. Dermott's letter.

'DEAR MRS. MOORHOUSE,

'I wonder if I can claim the help of someone who is nearly a relative? My husband
was taken unwell yesterday. The doctor
came to see him, and said all he needed was
rest. This morning, however, he is rather
worse than better, and the doctor, who has
been here again, says Robert should be seen
by a heart specialist at once. Would it be too
much to ask you to try to find one for us,
and send him back in the carriage...?'

Here Mrs. Dermott mentioned the specialist of her choice, but begged Bel if he were
not immediately available to find one who
would come at once. The carriage was at her
disposal.

There was nothing to be done, then, but to
accede to Mrs. Dermott's request. A few
hurried inquiries as to the state of the house,
a quick look round in the hall, an assurance
shouted by Phœbe from an upper landing
that everything was all right; and Bel found
herself sitting in the Dermotts' family
carriage, heading once more in the direction
of the town.

Ten minutes later she was in the region of
Charing Cross and Crescents, and the
horses were swinging round towards New-
ton Terrace, which was then, as it still in part
is, Glasgow's Harley Street.

No – Sir Hamish was not at home, a discreet male servant told Bel. At this hour he was, as usual, at the Royal Infirmary. Yes, it would be worth her while if she could drive straight there. But would the lady wait one moment? – and he would ask Sir Hamish's colleague on the Bell telephone; just to make certain of Sir Hamish's movements. Bel stood in the hall wondering, while the man went to a little box placed on a bracket on the wall. He spoke a number, waited, then entered into what seemed to be a conversation, although Bel could only hear his side of it. At the end of this he turned to Bel, and, as though he had merely been interrogating a third person, informed her that she was certain to find Sir Hamish at the Royal Infirmary if she went. He was likely to be there for still another half-hour.

The great man's door, with its glossy green paint and its shining letter-box, closed behind her, as she hurried down the steps, gave the waiting footman fresh directions, and settled back inside.

III

Bel stood in the square in front of the Royal Infirmary, her task accomplished. The name of Robert Dermott had had its effect on Sir Hamish's augustness. He must, he felt, get himself to his dear and influential friend's bedside without delay. She stood watching the carriage swing round into Mason Street and disappear, the coachman whipping up the horses as much as he dare in the City's traffic. She had delivered her message with decorum, and what she hoped was elegant dignity, and, even at this anxious moment, some enjoyment of the sense of her own importance. Sir Hamish had, very civilly, offered her a lift westward. But she had declined it, insisting that she must put no kind of hindrance in his way.

Now, as she stood under the portico of the hospital, she found herself wondering what next she had better do. She had gathered, in the brief moment she stood inside her own house, that Phœbe and the maids had dealt with the ravages of Saturday. There was nothing immediate to do, then, at Grosvenor Terrace. The excitement of finding the doctor and sending him off to Aucheneame had driven David and his problem from her mind, but now, in the blank left by the specialist's departure, her midday meeting had come back to her. What was she to do with David? How was she to help him?

Presently it occurred to her that she might go down to see her mother. It was not far, and she would be glad, now, of the air. She took her way down the Bell o' the Brae, down the High Street and Saltmarket to the

248

gates of Glasgow Green on purpose to walk across the Park to Monteith Row.

Her mother received her with some surprise. She had expected that Bel would be engaged in putting her house to rights. 'I didna expect to see ye today,' she said, as she sat her daughter down and rang for the inevitable cup of tea.

'No, I had to go to the Royal Infirmary.'

'The Royal Infirmary?'

Bel explained. The old lady shook her grey side-curls with much rueful gusto. 'If it's heart it's a bad business, I doubt.' And then, after a pause, 'Will the money go straight to David's wife?'

'I've no idea, Mother. But we all hope the old man will live.'

But Mrs. Barrowfield would have none of it. Again she shook her head, and insisted that if it was heart it was sure to be a bad business. Bel was so used to her mother's habit of killing off her contemporaries, that she did not bother to protest further. Tea was being brought in, so she allowed her mother to ply her with questions about the concert before old Maggie.

When the door was finally closed behind them, she came to the reason of her visit.

'I've something I want to talk to you about, Mother. I met David at lunch-time today. He says he's fallen in love with Lucy Rennie.'

Bel saw that Mrs. Barrowfield had, after the fashion of the elderly, not bothered to take this in. She poured out tea and merely said, 'Now, sugar it for yourself,' as she handed Bel her cup. Her daughter knew she must give her time. 'Did ye say ye saw David?' she said presently.

'Yes, Mother, I'm telling you. I saw him today. He's fallen in love with Lucy Rennie.'

Mrs. Barrowfield stirred her tea. 'But surely he's in love with Miss Dermott, is he not?' she said, with what looked like a maddening determination to misunderstand.

'That's the whole trouble, Mother. That's what I've come to talk to you about. He wants to break his engagement.'

'Who's this Lucy Rennie?' Mrs. Barrowfield put down her cup.

'The girl who sang on Saturday. David knew her when they were children.'

'And he says he's in love with her?'

'Yes.'

'And what about Miss Dermott?'

'Yes. What about her, Mother?'

The old lady sat thinking. The facts had penetrated. Bel waited.

'When was the marriage to be?' she asked at length.

'The beginning of March.'

Again Mrs. Barrowfield lapsed into silence. When she spoke again, her tone was hot with contempt – the contempt of an old squaw, who cannot forgive disloyalty to the tribe.

'David Moorhouse is a terrible fool!'

'It doesn't help to say that, Mother.'

'Fancy jilting Robert Dermott's girl for somebody like that!'

'I don't think he's thrown her over yet, Mother. I've advised him to do nothing until her father's better.' Somehow her mother's implication that David was letting a fortune slip annoyed Bel. Had she been quite honest with herself, she would have realised that this aspect of the matter worried her, too. But there was so much more than that. She liked David, and she liked Grace. She applauded what they stood for. David's folly was more to her than a mere business deal going wrong.

'I've always got on with David,' Mrs. Barrowfield continued. 'He was a bit bee-headed, when he was young. But I thought he had got over all that.'

'What am I to do, mother? He asked for my help.'

'Is this woman still in Glasgow?'

'She's going away in the middle of this week.'

'Ye canna keep him away from her, I suppose?'

'Not if he wants to go.'

The old woman thought again for a moment, then said, 'He should be down at the Dermotts', where they need him. He'll know Miss Dermott's father's ill?'

'They would send word to the office.'

'Ye better go up to his lodgings on yer way home and make sure.' Mrs. Barrowfield got up, pulled her fine white shawl about her shoulders and moved about the room. She was furious with David. She stopped at her window looking across the Green, which was beginning to be lost in the growing dusk and the fog rising from the river. She was turning matters over in her slow, but not stupid mind. This Dermott-Moorhouse alliance would be good for all the Moorhouse family, and, therefore, good for her daughter, who was one of them. At last she turned.

'Well, there's just this about it, Bel,' she said. 'I've known David a long time, and I've always liked him. But he's not what ye would call a strong character. If ye could just get him married to Miss Dermott, it wouldna break his heart that he hadna married the other one.'

'That's what I think, Mother. I got his promise to wait for a day or two, anyway.'

'Aye. The great thing is to get him to wait. It can make all the difference. And there's always old Robert Dermott's illness to send him back to Robert Dermott's daughter. Be sure ye see that he knows about it tonight.'

Bel called at David's rooms an hour later.

As she did not find him there, she asked leave to come in and write him an urgent message.

Chapter Nineteen

On this same Monday, when so much else was happening, Lucy Rennie spent most of the day packing. She was sick of Glasgow and all it stood for – so sick, indeed, that she had decided to leave it a day earlier than she had planned. She wished, now, that she had not been so obliging as to stay over for Mrs. Arthur Moorhouse's concert. People like the Moorhouses did not deserve to be noticed by artists.

In allowing herself these reactions, Lucy was not quite just. She was deliberately choosing to forget that it was she who had first proposed the concert to Mrs. Moorhouse, with the object of helping, a little, the distress that was at the moment so widely spread in the city. But now she was in reaction from the effort she had put forth, and she was ready to blame, merely for the relief of blaming.

The truth of it was that her vanity as a musician had been hurt. Though, had she been faced with this, she probably would have denied it. She had had success. People had applauded, and called her back to sing more. That was, of course, gratifying, but just what her experience had expected. Her practised eye had seen at a glance that this well-dressed, well-fed, well-circumstanced audience would clap its good-natured, indiscriminating hands at anything which conformed to its conventions. And it certainly was better that they should clap them than not clap them. But somehow, when everything was over, when these noisy, wealthy people had stood about drinking tea and chatting with their acquaintance, she – the singer, the centre of this meeting, who had given her voice, her skill and her forces – had been allowed to stand aside unnoticed.

Wealthy, place-seeking Glasgow had milled about the room, teacup in hand, the lesser seeking out the greater, in the hope of catching a wan smile of recognition or a crumb of conversation.

Or so it seemed to Lucy, who was well used to metropolitan drawing-rooms. She, a Scot herself, had forgotten the Scots' reticence, the fear of addressing an artist, lest the word of praise might seem an impertinence. She could think of other private recitals in the South, where people had come to her, wrung her hand, and talked a deal of flattering nonsense. But for one who had given of her best it was better that way. It let down strung-up nerves and gave a sense of release and relaxation.

Mrs. Arthur Moorhouse should have seen to all this. After all, she, Lucy Rennie, should have been singled out. Instead of that, Mrs. Moorhouse had shown signs of being fussed, of letting the reins slip from her hands. One pompous woman after another had borne down on the hostess, who had lost control, and allowed herself to become enveloped. She had, indeed, bestowed flustered thanks on Lucy when she said goodbye. But that had been all, except for a short and, Lucy thought, gauche little note, thanking Miss Rennie in a perfunctory way, telling her of the gratifying sum collected, and hoping formally that any time Miss Rennie found herself in Glasgow, she would come to Grosvenor Terrace to see them.

And David Moorhouse? Now, this evening, as Lucy sat musing in her gaudy little sitting-room, she wondered if David were not, after all, at the core of her unhappiness. He was so obviously attracted to her. It was absurd and disturbing. After all, the young woman he had promised to marry in some six or seven weeks' time had been there, at the concert, too.

Lucy rose, and drew the heavy fringed curtains to shut out the last of the foggy, dying twilight. The room was warmer so, with no other light now but the flickerings of the fire, as they threw up weird, dancing shadows on the walls. It would be very easy, really, for her to become sentimental over David Moorhouse – to remind herself that they had promised to be sweethearts as children after the fashion of magazine stories. Yet this young man appealed to her. He had no artistic sensibilities. But he was gentle and quick. She had noticed more than once a sudden flush and a sharp question in David's eyes, when he feared for a moment that his talk had been construed wrongly, feared he had given pain. Add to that his pleasant good looks and the springtime memories of childhood, and it would not be difficult to let oneself go. Lucy stared at the flames. Now she was asking herself a direct question. If David were free and asked her to marry him, what would she have to say to him? It was a pity she had not known him as a grown man sooner. They might have done very well together, and it might have saved her from more than one male friendship that she would, by Moorhouse, or, indeed, by any other standards, have been better without.

Now she could hear the little door-bell clanging on its spring in the kitchen. Then footsteps. It must be her landlord home from work. She looked about her and sighed. No. There was no question of herself and David Moorhouse. So why bother to think about it? She had weathered storms enough already. Her heart would not be broken.

II

The door of her little sitting-room was thrown open.

'Mr. David Moorhouse.'

Lucy rose. Her training had taught her cool-headedness. But for a moment her face was flooded with colour, and she found herself fighting down confusion.

'David!'

He seemed as perturbed as she was. 'I'm sorry if I've disturbed you, Lucy. I had to see you before you went away.' He closed the door behind him, and stood for a moment against it, one hand behind his back still holding the handle. The flickering firelight caught lights in his chestnut hair, lit up his face, and flung a fantastic shadow of him on the wall beyond.

She was getting possession of herself. 'Come and sit down.' She forced a laugh. 'Don't stand there, as if I were going to eat you.'

He came forward, threw his hat on the table and sat down on the other side of the hearth.

It was Lucy who spoke first, after a moment of bewildered silence. 'Shall I light the gas?'

'The fire's all right.' He was tense, unnatural. He might say anything.

She had had declarations before. If he
must speak, he had better do so. She bent
down and stirred the fire. 'There,' she said,
'that's a bit brighter. Take off your overcoat.'

He paid no attention to this invitation. He
merely sat, fumbling with the gloves he held
in his hand. 'When do you go?' he asked
presently.

'Tomorrow morning, David. I have nothing to keep me. And I've work waiting in
London.'

'I'm glad I came up this evening.'

There was nothing to reply to this. She
would neither help nor hinder what he had
to say. She allowed her eyes to wander back
to the fire.

'Lucy.'

She turned towards him. He was trying
with difficulty to say something.

'Yes, David?'

'Lucy, if I were free to marry you, would
you marry me?' He spoke the words ex-
plosively. She saw that his eyes were great
with excitement; that his hands were wring-
ing the gloves he held until they looked like
pieces of rope.

She stood up and began to pace the room.
He rose, too, as though to follow her.

'No, David. Stay where you are. Let me

think.' She came back to the mantelpiece, and stood looking down upon him. 'Have you broken with Grace Dermott?' she asked presently.

'No. I promised I wouldn't do anything for a day or two. Her father's ill.'

'Promised? Promised whom?' She could see that, with the sharpness of her question, he regretted his last words already.

'I've been very unhappy about this, Lucy.'

'But have you discussed me with Miss Dermott?'

'Oh no. With Bel. I thought she could help me.'

'What had *she* to do with it?'

'Lucy, perhaps you don't understand. I've always been a close friend of Bel's. Ever since I was a very young man.'

'So this is a matter for the whole Moor-house family?'

'Oh no, Lucy. Bel's the only one who knows.'

She stood, gazing into the fire, one hand on the draped mantelpiece, one foot on the wrought-iron fender, her other hand catching up her dress as it rested on her knee. She was trembling with anger. So this had already been dragged before the Moorhouses? What did it matter if it were only Bel Moorhouse? She was the distilled essence of all of them – the distilled essence of everything that was complacent and Philistine; of everything that she, Lucy Rennie, had been forced to fight against.

But now, in the lightning of her rage, Lucy saw clearly that she loved this young man, whose background she detested.

When she spoke, her voice was hot with passion, with the echoes of old rebellions, with the desire to wound.

'You don't happen to be in love with me, David, do you?'

'Of course! I–'

'Well, you haven't said so.'

'Lucy – please! That's why I'm here, against–'

'Against your better judgment, David? "Your purer self"?'

'You're trying to hurt me.'

'But you don't mind hurting me, do you?'

'I didn't know I was ever going to meet anyone like you, when I got engaged.'

'And now you want to make the best of both worlds, David?'

'I don't know what you mean.'

'You want to make quite sure that you're on with me, before you do anything so rash as to break with Grace Dermott. You've decided all this carefully with your sister-in-law. Oh, you're smug! Smug and hard and cowardly! All of you!'

David stood up in alarm. Lucy had burst into a fit of sobbing, and was standing beside him shaking, her face in her hands.

'Lucy! Lucy! What can I say to make you believe me?'

'Believe what?' She was standing looking up at him with brimming eyes. He could feel her willing him to take her into his arms. He caught her up, and kissed her with such a kiss as he had never given before. It was his turn to tremble now, in the tempest of his feelings. Here there was no room for calculated thought, for solemn promises to himself of honourable behaviour – room for nothing but his staggering senses.

At last she disengaged herself. 'David, what are we doing?'

She could have done now what she would with him, and this knowledge staunched, in part, her wounded pride. But a common liaison with David Moorhouse was not her purpose.

'You haven't given me a reply, Lucy.'

The tone of his voice touched her. She must thrust this untimely, passionate anger from her, search her feelings, and make her decision with as much coolness as she could. 'David, dear – no. Sit down again. Have patience with me. Let me think for a moment.'

'Then you will consider what I'm asking?'

'Hush!' She took up again her former attitude by the mantelpiece. No. She must make David jump through every one of the hoops of his own conventionality, in order to come to her. Her pride would allow nothing else.

'David,' she said at length, 'so long as you're engaged to Miss Dermott, I can't possibly discuss this matter with you. I was wrong to let you kiss me just now. Now please go, before there's any more foolishness.'

'Lucy, you're not angry?'

'No, David. I'm not angry.'

'Can I write to you?'

'If you have anything to write about.' She turned, gave him a card bearing her address in London, then held out her hand. 'Goodbye, David. And God bless you.'

He took her hand, repeated 'God bless you', picked up his hat and went.

III

David made his way down Hill Street without knowing what he did. Last night, Grace. Now tonight, Lucy. And yet he had always considered himself rather more than usually self-possessed. What had happened? He must be mad. Instinct would have taken him back to Bel, but a moment of thought showed him that this way was barred.

And yet, if Bel could have come on David as he stood now, aimlessly at the corner of Cambridge Street, looked into his heart, and glimpsed the depths of his trouble, she would, loving him as she did, have been torn for him as she would have been torn for one of her own sons.

David stood dazed, looking about him in the foggy, ill-lit darkness. Then, as no tram-car appeared, he turned and, thrusting his hands deep into his greatcoat pockets, made his way towards the lights of Sauchiehall Street. Presently he became aware that an arm was being pushed through his own. He stopped to look round. It was his friend Stephen Hayburn.

'Stephen!'

Stephen smiled. 'I've been watching you for quite a long time. I even spoke to you, but you didn't notice me. Anything wrong, David?'

David stood still, merely giving Stephen a nod of recognition. 'Many things are wrong with me tonight,' he said at length, 'but I can't talk about them.'

'Anything I can do?'

'Yes. Take me somewhere.'

'Have you had something to eat, David?'

'No.'

Stephen went with David, wondering. Had he broken with Grace Dermott? Was he in debt? Had he got himself into some doubt-ful tangle? He had known David for the bet-ter part of ten years, and he knew that such happenings were much more likely to befall himself than anyone so respectable as a

Moorhouse. They had both been frivolous in their early twenties together, but for years now David had been the mirror of propriety.

'Where do you want to go?'

'Anywhere you like, Stephen.'

Presently David and Stephen found themselves in a little foreign eating-house at the City end of Sauchiehall Street. It was steamy and warm, and smelt pleasantly of Mediterranean cooking. A dark-eyed waiter, with a white apron round his waist, welcomed Stephen as a friend, and led the young men across the sawdust floor. They settled themselves and looked about them. The little restaurant, with its coarse table-cloths, wooden pepper-mills and toothpicks, was busy with Glasgow's Bohemia. A couple of heavy-bearded German fiddlers were, each of them, wolfing plates of macaroni, and drinking the pale beer of their own country from high glasses: players, probably, from some orchestra. Argentine Spaniards from shipping-offices chattered noisily over their specially cooked tortilla and their raw, Iberian wine. A bedizened lady with saffron curls, talking bad French, was being entertained by a swarthy but fashionable southern Italian, who was managing his macaroni with an elegance that should have put the Germans to shame. The place was ridiculous, cosmopolitan and gay.

Stephen sat back preparing to enjoy himself. But his companion, he saw, was pre-

264

occupied and listless. When their friend the waiter returned with his thumbed little menu card, Stephen sent him at once to fetch a flagon of wine.

'There. Put that down,' he said, pouring David a full glass from the round, straw-covered bottle.

As he had intended, food and much wine began to have their effect. David was beginning to look like himself. Presently he was even commenting with some amusement on the people about him.

'Well, David, feeling better?'

'Yes. Glad I met you.'

'You wouldn't like to tell me what was troubling you?'

David shook his head. 'I can't,' was all he said.

Stephen tried to read his flushed face, but could discover nothing. 'Well, never mind,' he said.

Stephen Hayburn's thoughts went back some months to the time when the Hayburn fortunes had gone in the Glasgow City Bank disaster – a happening which had killed his mother. David had been kind then. He would try to help him now.

IV

They were finishing their meal.

265

'What should we do? I don't want to go home,' David said rather surprisingly. No, he was looking almost cheerful.

'You're not drunk, are you?'

'No. But I feel better than I did.'

Stephen looked at his watch and considered. 'It's after eight. I say – we haven't been to Brown's music-hall together for years.'

'We'll still get in. It's Monday night. I forget who's performing, but anyway we'll be in time for the nine o'clock ballet.'

The two young men made their way down the hill and across George's Square to Dunlop Street. As Stephen had predicted, there was no difficulty in getting into Brown's, even at this hour. Monday evening was slack. The little music-hall was gay enough, although there was less tobacco smoke and noise than David seemed to remember. He wondered what the family would think of him. In the early days he had received more than one lecture from Arthur for coming here. Places like Brown's were not approved of.

A massive lady in a dress of black sequins, white, elbow-length kid-gloves, and a white rose in her piled-up, ginger hair, was singing sentimentally in a loud contralto, as Stephen and David made their way to the bar at the back, and stood waiting for her turn to finish, that they might order their drink and find a seat. When at length they came down towards the front, the chairman spied Stephen and waved to him with his wooden mallet. Presently David found himself sitting in the chairman's half-circle in front of the grand piano and the little orchestra.

Now the chairman was knocking for silence. He was announcing the next item. This was fantastic, unreal. David was in possession of his wits, but his senses were misted. This circle of boisterous men. Those busy musicians. The curtain with its tinsel fringe reflecting the flickerings of the foot-lights. And now this ridiculous little street scene, with a jaunty Cockney telling them in his song that he was in love with a lady called 'Clementina Angelina Margarita Green', who had unaccountable ways of fainting in situations which became more and more compromising as verse succeeded verse. Fantastic, unreal. But he was laugh-ing with the others. Inside, he was bruised, perhaps, but it didn't matter.

The song came to its first ending in a storm of laughter and applause, and the jaunty comedian, having run out and in to the roll of the drum, at length let himself be persuaded to stay and sing the naughtiest verse of all. Now that, too, was over, and after more clapping the curtain closed and the lights went up once more.

'Have another drink, David?'

David declined. His Moorhouse caution had decided that for the moment he had had enough. Stephen went off to get a drink for himself. Before he could get back the ballet had begun. Six young ladies in black-and-yellow-striped tights and wearing gauze wings representing, presumably, bees, set themselves prettily to pursue six more, who were even more colourful, and represented butterflies. When this dance came to an end, and the Queen Bee and the King of the Butterflies, also a lady, were falling into postures ready to begin their part of the revels, Stephen, who had slipped back into his seat, turned to David:

'There's a lady friend of yours here tonight.'

'Here? Who?' David was puzzled. He was not the kind of young man to have lady friends in the half-world of Glasgow. And the women of his family and their like would rather die than be seen in a place like this.

'Tell you after.' Stephen was giving his whole attention now to the gyrations of the Queen Bee and the Butterfly King.

The ballet ended at last, and the voluptuously curved ladies minced back more than once to receive the applause that was their due. Again David pressed his question.

For reply, Stephen rose, took his arm and said, 'Come on, it's time you had another drink. Whether you want it or not. You'll probably meet her.'

And so it came about that David, carrying a full glass in the promenade of the little theatre, came, once more, face to face with Lucy Rennie. At a later time he could not tell why the encounter gave him this sense of shock. Tonight he had left Hill Street, his mind torn with indecision, self-hatred and amazement. Amazement that his senses had driven him to make the offer he had made. By his meeting with Stephen, he had managed to lay his stunned distress aside for a time.

Now, here was the ground in front of him burst open, and the same Lucy, provocative and very much mistress of the situation, smiling up at him. There was nothing extraordinary about her except that she was here, in this place which all Moorhouses regarded as a resort of libertines and scarlet women. Here, taking everything complacently for granted. Her arm was linked through the arm of the man who had accompanied her singing in Bel's drawing-room.

'Well, David? I didn't expect to find you here in this frivolous place.' There was sympathy and, somehow, an echo of the intimacy of their meeting earlier in the evening. But no sense of embarrassment.

'This is my friend Stephen Hayburn, Lucy. He brought me. I haven't been here for years.'

There were introductions and easy laughter. Lucy explained how she had felt so dull that when her friend had called to say goodbye, she had asked him to take her somewhere gay.

David did not know what to make of it. Had his conventionality seen Lucy as quite another person? Had it allowed him no understanding? Could the standards of his life offer his feelings no yardstick, that Lucy's presence here so much disturbed him? Or was he just a prig? A fool?

The music had struck up again. The curtain had parted, and a juggler and his lady were getting ready to perform wonders. Stephen and Lucy's cavalier had moved ahead.

Lucy turned to David. 'There's lots of room tonight. We can all sit together.'

They found places to one side, and sat watching the remainder of the performance. David was glad when it came to an end. He felt unhappy and ridiculous. Why did he so ardently hope that no one who mattered should see him here? What was this un-explained sense of shame? Why did it dis-please him that Lucy seemed so much at her ease?

At the entrance she gave him her hand, telling him that her friend, who lived near her, would see her to her lodgings. Confused, bewildered and heartsick, David bade Stephen goodnight, and took his way home.

There were two short notes waiting for him on his sitting-room table. One was from Bel saying she had called, and regretting she had missed him. The other was from Grace, delivered by the hand of a servant. They both contained the same message. Robert Dermott's condition had become very serious. David was to go to Grace and her mother at once.

Chapter Twenty

It was curious that it did not occur to David that he should not now go to Aucheneame; that, with his visit to Lucy, this evening, and with what had happened, he must have given up the right to enter Robert Dermott's house as the promised husband of Robert Dermott's daughter. He sat down heavily in his armchair by the dying fire, crushing the two pieces of paper in his hand. His quick sympathy could feel Grace's present distress, and he was sharply aware of how much she must need him. It was too late to go tonight, but tomorrow morning he would take an early train. His head had become clear, but it had cleared merely to show him his own perplexities. On the one hand he felt as though Grace's eyes were fixed upon him, accusing him of frivolity, and worse, while her father's life was in danger; and, on the other, it was as though he could see Lucy's smile of mockery, that he, a man of thirty-one, could not take himself and his emotions in hand and behave before the world with courage and honesty. Lucy had been right, of course, to refuse to give him an answer so long as he was promised to Grace. Yet Grace's father was ill, and, as Bel insisted, he must not be so cruel as to break with her now. But yet again, he had felt he must speak to Lucy before she disappeared from Glasgow. Now he could well see that it must have looked to her as though he had wanted to make sure of her before he had finally broken with Grace. He could see how despicable he must have seemed.

But was it not more than a seeming? Was it not, indeed, true? Still in his overcoat in the cold sitting-room, David sat forward staring before him. Had his cautious Moorhouse instincts been at work? Or was it that somewhere at the bottom of his heart he had no real intention of giving up Grace Dermott? Yet what had driven him to Lucy's room this evening? And had something changed in himself since he had seen this other Lucy in Brown's, later tonight? A new Lucy, familiar, easy and undisturbed among the light-headed, none too well-behaved men, in a place where even his independent and unconventional sister Phœbe would never have gone. Was he beginning to realise that Lucy Rennie lived by a different code from his own?

It was in the small hours of the morning that David stirred himself from his chair to go to bed. He would lie down, even if he did not sleep. Tomorrow, events must be his counsellors. He would go, at least, and help these two women in their distress. He was, he knew, the only man they had to turn to.

He was actually asleep when his landlady roused him early to a foggy, wet morning. His body was numb and weary and consciousness, as it returned to him, brought with it all the confusion and dilemma of the night. But now, however weary he might feel, he must face what lay before him. Robert Dermott's wife and daughter would already be wondering, indeed, why he was not with them.

He got up hurriedly, shivering, as he poured the hot shaving-water from the polished metal can into his wash-basin. The air, even in his bedroom, was raw with a penetrating January dampness. His landlady, a homely creature with an affection for him, scolded him as she brought him his overcoat. He appeared to have eaten so little breakfast. The notes of last night, she told him, had been left, one by a man in livery, the other by a lady who had asked permission to come in and write; who had said she was Mr. David Moorhouse's sister-in-law. The lady had seemed disturbed. Nothing, the good woman hoped, was wrong. Miss Dermott's father was ill, David told her, as he hurried away.

It was not the first time, David reflected, looking out upon the sodden, misty country from his railway carriage, that he had gone down to Aucheneame in a state of emotional tension. His mind went back to the day of his engagement to Grace, and from that his thoughts went on to review everything that followed. At Aucheneame he had found much happiness, and much contentment; a conventionality that suited him very well, and peace of mind. Grace had spoken his own language, and he had fallen into a well-bred fondness for her, which had promised nothing but good in the closer intimacy of marriage. If only his heart had not been astonished into this folly with Lucy Rennie. In the passionless grey of the winter morning, David sighed and called himself a fool.

The train halted at a half-way station down the river. David became aware that a watery sun had broken through. Wet roofs and roadways were gleaming in a chill January light. His one companion in the carriage, a businessman who had sat throughout reading the morning news, jumped up, asked the name of the station, hurriedly threw down his paper and got out. The train started once more on its way.

David's thoughts had been far from newspapers, but now, seeking perhaps to escape his troubles for an instant, he picked up this one left in the seat, and ran his eyes down its front page.

Thus it was that he learnt that Robert Dermott was dead.

II

In some minutes more the train had reached its destination. David found himself, the only passenger to alight, standing on the country platform. For an instant he stood stupidly looking about him. The stationmaster blew his whistle, waved his flag and the train puffed off on its leisurely morning journey down the riverside. The tide was low. A light western breeze was coming up from the Firth, smelling of mud-flats, sand and seawrack. Above his head a seagull wheeled and cried querulously in the pale sunshine.

'Your ticket, sir?'

'Oh yes. Of course.'

'Many thanks.' The stationmaster, knowing David now by sight, touched his cap to

the young man who was to marry Robert
Dermott's daughter.

'There's naebody tae meet ye, sir.' This
was strange, the man thought. Surely the
Dermott household, even on this sad morning, must know the movements of so close a
friend and send a carriage to fetch him from
the station.

'It's all right, thanks. They didn't quite
know when I would come.'

David set off towards Aucheneame. He let
his legs take him in the direction of his duty.
Disjointed scraps of thought passed through
his mind as he walked. The obituary notice in
the morning paper. 'Mr. Dermott's sudden
death would be a severe loss to the shipping
world.' 'A man of great ability, and a staunch
supporter of the City's charities.' Discreet,
unstressed details of Robert Dermott's
humble beginnings. 'Mr. Dermott's daughter
and only child is engaged to Mr. David
Moorhouse, a young Glasgow businessman,
who, it is understood, has quite recently
entered the firm of Dermott Ships Limited.'
Scraps from the music-hall performance of
last night. His hurrying footsteps were patter-
ing out the rhythm of 'Clementina Angelina
Margarita Green'. The absurd, tripping
ballet. Lucy's face. 'Well, David, I didn't
expect to find you here, in a frivolous place
like this.' The visit to Lucy's rooms. 'Goodbye, David. And God bless you.' No; events

had arranged themselves wrong. Nothing made sense. Perhaps sometime in the future the knots would come out of their tangle, and he would find rest.

There was Aucheneame now, with its blinds lowered in mourning. He gazed up at the great house as it stood up stark among its low shrubberies. He felt as though he wanted to ask it a question. But the lowered blinds made it look like a face with closed eyes; impassive and refusing to respond. He hurried on, his feet crushing the new-raked gravel of the drive. In another moment he had ascended the short flight of steps to the front door and was ringing the bell.

He has received by a man-servant with discreet surprise and pleasure. 'We didn't know when you would get here, sir.'

'I got back very late last night. I only got the message to come, then.'

At David's request the man followed him into a room while he asked him questions. Robert Dermott had died in the early evening, while Sir Hamish was in the house. It had been too late to find David at Dermott Ships Limited, and he was not to be found at his rooms. The ladies, as was natural, were stunned by the event, but Miss Grace had left word that she was to be told at once of his arrival. She was now in her room, but there was no doubt that she would want to see him. She had been awaiting his arrival with impatience. The man went, leaving David alone.

The lowered blinds with the sun upon them made a strange yellow twilight in the room, giving the appearance of things an unreality. David stood in front of the new-lit fire waiting, listening intently. This house of mourning seemed strangely silent: a muffled whisper; the crack of a floor-board now and then. That was all. A sparrow chirped outside in the shrubbery. Now he was aware of his own heart-beats, beating out the rhythm 'Clementina Angelina Margarita Green'. No. It was preposterous. He'd think about all that later – later, when he was not a mere mechanism, here to do what was expected of him.

Presently the door opened softly and Grace came to him. Now that she was here, it seemed natural that he should have come to help her. There were traces of fatigue and weeping, but her pleasure at seeing him had made her almost radiant. Her dress, even, was familiar, for she had not yet had time to secure mourning.

'David, darling. There you are. We've been trying to find you.' She was sobbing with relief as he held her in his arms.

Now she was sitting beside him possessively holding his hand and giving him a controlled account of her father's last hours; of Sir Hamish's arrival, and of his inability to do anything in the face of Robert Dermott's condition.

Presently she was leading David to her father's room. The old Highlander lay under a white sheet, his arms crossed on his breast. Grace's mother rose from a chair by the bedside, and embraced David, weeping. Her daughter scolded her gently for not resting and led her away.

Left alone with this man who had accomplished so much, who, for once, would deserve the formal words that would be spoken and printed in his praise, David was surprised to find himself invaded by a sense of calmness. In the quiet immensity of death, his own confusions seemed to recede from him, to fall into proportion. Here, too, it was so still that, as he stood at the foot of Robert Dermott's bed, he could again feel his tired pulses throbbing. But this time the throbbing did not beat out the words of a song. Now Grace, her hand in his own, was standing looking with him at her father. It was almost with a feeling of reluctance that he allowed her at last to draw him away.

'Come, David. We've got things to see about.'

III

In the little room where Robert Dermott had been used to conduct his personal business, Grace gave David his keys.

'But, Grace, is it right that I should know about your father's affairs?'

'He wanted it. He said so yesterday. There's a letter for you, in his desk.'

David turned the key in the great office desk, and slid back its heavy top. As he had expected, everything was arranged in order. Papers relating to the house, the garden and the stables were neatly docketed and carefully classified. There were receipts and personal correspondence. Together they sought out and found Robert Dermott's letter, the sealed envelope, addressed in a careful, almost copperplate hand: a hand that had been acquired with much diligence by an ambitious Highland boy, whose dream it had been to come out of the mountains and seek his fortune in the City. It bore the words: 'To my son-in-law, David Moorhouse. To be opened in the event of my death', and was dated 1st January, 1879. The letter ran as follows:

'MY DEAR DAVID,

'I am sitting in the quiet of the New Year's morning thinking of my family. I am not a young man now, and in times past I have worried about my wife and daughter. I just want to tell you that your engagement to Grace, and everything I have come to know of you since, has lifted a weight from my mind. It is a great relief for me to know that I now have a son in whom I can have full confidence; I need not recommend my dear ones to your care and your affection. The cashier of Dermott Ships Limited has my will and all instructions locked up in my private drawer in his safe at the office. The key is with the others on my ring. May God bless you all. I hope I shall have lived to see a grandchild, before you open this letter.

'Yours affectionately,
'ROBERT DERMOTT.'

David put the letter down. Grace, who had been reading it over his shoulder as he sat, picked it up, and carrying it to a window, re-read it tearfully. With hands clasped on the desk in front of him, David sat staring vacantly at the row of pigeon-holes before him. He was conscious of a great weariness now, conscious that last night his unhappiness had allowed him little sleep. Yet, as he thought of the generous message to him set down in the old man's letter, he could not feel the shackles it was laying upon him, as he might have done yesterday. Something had changed within him. Perhaps, if he did what he conceived to be his duty, his perplexities would begin to fade away and leave him at peace.

There was an early meal, in order that David should get back to the office in the afternoon to seek help in making funeral arrangements. In the evening he promised to be with Grace and her mother once more.

As he made his way back to Glasgow, David lay back in the empty carriage and closed his eyes. The wheels were beating steadily beneath him. There would be wheels beating steadily beneath Lucy Rennie at this moment as the day train to London hammered out the long miles. Yesterday, after he had left her in Hill Street, he had felt certain that, before long, he would be in the train too, following her, seeking her out. But now he was not sure.

He hadn't Lucy Rennie's courage. Her ability to throw away the substance for the shadow. He'd never understand that for the Lucy Rennies the shadows are everything.

As he passed up the street to the offices of Dermott Ships Limited, he stopped to buy himself a new black cravat, asking permission to tie it in the shop. Was his vanity stirring to life? Did he feel that he, David Moorhouse, could not escape a gratifying importance in the eyes of the staff as he made his first entrance as a mourner.

At the great swing-doorway of the offices, a senior clerk who chanced to be coming out stood aside, holding it open to let him pass, and giving him a greeting pregnant with condolence and respect. As he passed through to the chairman's room, Stephen

Hayburn came forward, gave him his hand, said he was sorry to hear the news, and withdrew tactfully.

The elder men of the staff, some of whom had shared Robert Dermott's struggles, came to shake his hand. He could see that their sorrow was sincere. It had not been difficult to like the old man. David, as he returned their handshakes, was full of understanding, earnest solemnity and dignified regret. He unbent sympathetically and gave them such details of the chairman's death as they might want to have, and told them that the condition of the chairman's wife and daughter was what might be expected. As the seniors of the firm went back to their desks, they agreed that Mr. Moorhouse was feeling this death in a way that did him credit; that he was a fine young man, even if he hadn't anything like the brains and drive of the old man; and they felt, with some confidence, that there was no reason why, with such excellent support as themselves, Mr. Moorhouse and the firm of Dermott Ships Limited should not continue together on their prosperous way.

Late in the afternoon Arthur paid a visit. As he entered the chairman's room, hat in hand, David caught himself wondering if even his downright brother was not now showing him some slight deference. But he was glad to see Arthur, and stepped forward to greet him.

'I came in to see if there was anything we could do for ye, David.'

David thanked him, but thought not. Everything, with the help of the excellent people here, had been put in train.

'You'll be going back to Aucheneame tonight?' Arthur asked.

'Oh yes. They need me down there.'

'Bel was just saying she hoped this would-na keep back yer marriage for too long.'

'I don't think it will, Arthur. I'm ready when Grace is. It would be best now – for everybody.'

Chapter Twenty-One

In the first days of June, Charles Mungo Ruanthorpe-Moorhouse was born. The event occurred in the morning, and in the evening, before dinner, the baby's grandfather, Sir Charles, despite his eighty years and his indifferent health, eluded the vigilance of his lady, marched across to the Dower House of Duntrafford in pouring rain, broke through the ring of Margaret's attendants, and shook his exhausted daughter triumphantly by the hand. He told her she was a good girl, a credit to her parents, and reminded her with satisfaction that there was nothing the Ruanthorpes couldn't accomplish if they set their minds to it, the little red creature in the cradle before the fire being proof positive of this contention. He assured her that his life's wish had been fulfilled, and that now he was ready to die. Margaret opened her tired eyes for a moment, contemplated her father as he stood over her, saw his jacket dripping with rain, and decided it was very probable that he would not have long to wait. Sir Charles, however, turned on his heel, marched back home through the summer downpour, had a hot sitz-bath before his dressing-room fire, drank his grandson's health in champagne and Napoleon brandy, and settled down to a hilarious evening, declaring he had never felt so well in his life.

On the last Saturday of June the official celebrations were to take place. Tenantry and servants were to have sports in the Duntrafford park and receive a liberal meal in a large marquee set up for the occasion; while relatives of the family and such neighbouring gentry as came to pay their respects were to be given entertainment in Duntrafford House itself. In the evening there were to be fireworks.

The Glasgow members of the Moorhouse family looked to this event, each in a different fashion. On the surface, of course, everyone must appear delighted. But Bel, for one, couldn't help the feeling that a deal

285

too much fuss was being made about the Duntrafford baby. After all, she had safely brought three of her own into the world, sound in wind and limb, without as much as a single match being put to a single squib on the occasion of their arrival. Margaret, of course, was forty, which was a hazardous age to be having a first child, but even so, surely one could be thankful for dangers past without marquees and gunpowder.

In addition, it was the end of June – just the time when most Glasgow matrons were in the throes of packing knives and forks, bedsheets and table-linen, and preparing to transfer their households to some seaside place on the Clyde for the months of July and August. To have to key oneself, one's husband and one's children up to garden-party pitch was altogether too much. Bel decided to have a sister-in-laws' tea-party to feel the family pulse.

'I just wanted to know what you all felt about this Duntrafford visit next Saturday, dears,' Bel said, smiling around her with an affectionate assurance, born of the conscious possession of fine eggshell china and the heaviest solid silver. 'I wondered if we couldn't just slip down some other day, and see Margaret and take the new baby a present. You see, we ourselves are going off to Brodick on the first of the month, and although, of course, it would be lovely to go to Duntrafford, it would be a dreadful rush.'

Sophia's ideas chimed with Bel's. 'Just what I was thinking, dear. William was just saying this morning he didn't know how in the world we were going to manage to get to Saltcoats this summer. The new girl I have has turned out so stupid. This year I have to do the actual packing as well as all the brain-work. But I just said to William, "Well, my dear boy, another year I've no intention..."'

It took Mary to stem the flood. She looked at Sophia severely. 'We can't be disrespect-ful to Sir Charles.' And not for the first time, Bel's town upbringing was at a loss before the almost feudal respect that these farmer's daughters still bore to someone who had been their father's landlord.

'I want to go,' Phœbe said shortly. She had, indeed, just returned from Duntrafford that morning.

Sophia laughed. 'Oh, you! We all know you. Young birds or beasts or babies. You can't keep away from them.' It was on the tip of her tongue to add: 'It's time that boy of yours married you and you had some of your own,' but she stopped herself in time, fearful of reproving looks from Bel or Mary.

Bel turned to her newest sister-in-law, Mrs. David Moorhouse. 'What do you think about it, dear?'

Grace had been looking at Phœbe. This beautiful, restless child had been the most difficult for her to understand of all the Moorhouse family. Good to the point of simplicity herself, Grace had been collecting evidence in Phœbe's favour, seeking to find reasons for liking her. Now it pleased her to hear Sophia say that the girl had a mania for the young and the helpless. Bel's question brought her back.

'I had a very kind letter from Lady Ruanthorpe. She asked mother and David and myself to stay at Duntrafford for the weekend. But you see mother doesn't much feel like being away from home just yet. Still, I feel David and I should go. I dare say we'll get back on Saturday night. The carriage can meet us in Glasgow and drive us back late to Aucheneame.'

Bel had to acknowledge herself defeated. Grace, although she was not yet married to David more than three months, was already her favourite sister-in-law. But this daughter of luxury could not be expected to understand the magnitude of an expedition such as the one proposed for Saturday. To see three children dressed in the best of everything, a husband looking suitably dignified, prosperous and impeccable, and oneself in the height of fashion; and to keep everyone, including oneself, looking their best for a long and tiring summer's day – this was an undertaking to tax the wit and purpose of any woman. But she had both wit and purpose. And she knew it. Very well. She would take her family to Duntrafford on Saturday. And she would see to it that they, the Arthur Moorhouses, were the best-dressed and most presentable family there.

II

The day of rejoicing was hot. Sir Charles had spent an anxious week, looking a hundred times a day from the windows of Duntrafford at threatening clouds or actually falling rain. But suddenly on Saturday morning the old man, as he sat up in bed breakfasting, saw that the weather had cleared, and that a hot June sun already high in the summer heavens was causing a steamy mist to rise from the parklands beyond the lawn, and was beginning to dry the sodden canvas of the great marquee. This was better. Sir Charles ordered his man to fetch him the tussore suit he had worn last when he was in India, chose a bright tie, and put them on with much satisfaction. His lady, wearing black spotted foulard and a large leghorn hat, wagged her ebony stick at him and went off into peals of eldritch laughter. Her husband merely growled, muttered something about her not being fit to have a grand-child, and marched out of the house to inspect the preparations, heedless of her cries that he should remember that the grass must still be very wet.

The morning was delicious. In the late Ayrshire June the spring still lingered. The foliage was become rich and deep, but it had not yet taken to itself the dark, glossy green of midsummer. Followed by his two old house spaniels, Sir Charles, his hands clasped behind his back, stumped about enjoying himself. Trestle-tables were being set up in the marquee by caterers' men. He told them that he thought it was ridiculous to be arranging them in this way; that they should be arranging them in that other way; then walked off, feeling he had shown these fellows who was in authority.

At the finely wrought-iron gates of his walled garden, he commanded his spaniels to sit and wait for him, peering back through the ornamental iron tracery at two despondent pairs of bloodshot eyes that looked up as though they had been excluded from Paradise; told them to be good doggies, and went on down the damp scented turf alleys to see that his gardeners had carried out his instructions. Even Sir Charles had little to complain of. This Ayrshire garden was a miracle of luxuriance refreshed. The herbaceous borders were lavishly splashing their colours against the sombre green of the old yew-trees. Early roses, the raindrops still upon them, were sparkling in the sun. Tubs of geraniums and hydrangeas had been brought out from under glass and set about to add to the riot. Fruit was beginning to shape itself on the apple-trees, trained against the south wall. Sir Charles went, exchanging greetings with his gardeners, examining the trimmed edges, and pulling up the odd weed that seems to appear from nowhere after a warm, wet night. With a parting word that the men had better keep their eyes open while the mob walked round this afternoon, he turned and left the garden.

At a distance he could see that luncheon guests were beginning to arrive: Mungo's relatives from Glasgow, probably. This was annoying. Was it that time already? He had meant to go round and say good morning to his grandson, and ask his daughter Margaret how she did. But now these Moorhouse women would be gibbering and swarming all over the place, and making a fuss over a baby who meant nothing much to them. There they were, all silks and feathers and parasols, emptying themselves out of the wagonette and chattering like magpies. His wife and his son-in-law were dealing with them. Well, let them. He would see them all at lunch. Sir Charles stalked round a rhododendron bush in full bloom, hurried down a path in the shrubbery and entered the house by a side door.

He found his butler in the pantry, and told

291

him to bring a glass of madeira to his dressing-room, the only place where, today, his privacy was secure against invasion. He sat down in an easy chair before the empty fireplace, sipping his wine and resting. He felt a little tired. After all, a man couldn't stay young for ever. But this wine was doing him good. Giving him heart, making him feel that life had treated him well. There had been Charlie's death, of course. But on this radiant day that belonged to his grandson, he must not feel bitter, even about Charlie. He rose, went to a drawer in his desk, took out a little daguerreotype photograph of his son, and sat down again to examine it. Charlie... Margaret, good girl, had just been doing everything that could be done to staunch that wound.

He still had half his wine to finish. It was comfortable and pleasant here. The warm scents of June were coming in through the open window; perhaps, if he closed his eyes for a little...

Lunch was announced, and after some waiting, Lady Ruanthorpe came to look for him. She found him sleeping in his chair.

'Charles! Wake up! We had no idea where you had got to.'

He opened his eyes slowly.

'What's that on the floor?' She saw that a little gilt square was lying at his feet, half hidden in the bearskin rug. She bent down, picked up the picture of her son, fumbled for her glasses and examined it silently for a time; then put it back in its drawer.

'Hurry, Charles,' was all she said. 'You're keeping everybody waiting.'

III

On the whole, it was a highly uncomfortable day for Mungo. At any time this bashful countryman loathed pedestals, and here he was on this hot afternoon set up, as he felt, for everyone's approval or derision. He, a farmer-tenant like the rest, had dared to marry the laird's daughter. And here were all the other tenants with their womenfolk to nudge and criticise and wonder. He was proud of his son, but before these strapping countrymen and their wives, some of whom were younger than himself, yet already had eight or nine stocky children to their credit, one single baby seemed no very great exhibition of the virility of a man of forty-four. And inevitably, because of Sir Charles's age, the management of the celebrations must fall on Mungo's shoulders. He was acutely conscious of eyes following him as he moved about gravely greeting friends, directing helpers, and receiving congratulations.

No. His wife was not out yet. But she was doing well, he was glad to say. Sir Charles had pushed on with the celebrations so as not to interfere with the hay-making in July. How were they all 'up bye'? And how were the young beasts coming on this year? Yes. There was the baby being carried across the park by the old Duntrafford nurse, Mrs. Crawford. His sister Sophia was with them. They must go and speak to her. They could cut across after the sack race had finished. What was that they were saying? Yes, it was difficult to hear, with the brass band making all that noise. Yes, and there was Mary too. No, no. He had to admit that his sisters Sophia and Mary were not as thin as they had been when they left the Laigh Farm to go to Glasgow. But, then, that was years ago, wasn't it? And they weren't so young, either. Besides, dear me, they were the mothers of growing families now.

In answer to a distant sign, Mungo gave his farmer friends apologetic, friendly nods and moved off in the direction of a great beech-tree beside the lawn. Beneath its shade, seated in cushioned basket-chairs, and with their old spaniels snapping flies at their feet, Sir Charles and Lady Ruanthorpe were holding court. Most of their communication was dumb show, for the brass band, stationed near them, was playing indefatigably with a loudness that made speech inaudible.

Mungo made a detour round the sack race, which was being energetically refereed by his sister Phœbe; pushed his way through another dozen or so of farm children squealing with excitement as they prepared to run the next race, balancing potatoes on spoons; looked into the marquee, where stout countrywomen were sitting gossiping together out of the sun, drinking tea, or feeding their smaller children, before the older and more boisterous ones should rush in after the children's part of the sports was over, and snatch the little ones' share. Seeing that some county people from another great house were bending over his parents-in-law in greeting, Mungo hung back in the shelter of the crowd until they had passed on. Now he was standing beside them, as, suddenly, the band stopped. It had been so loud that for a moment the party beneath the tree found itself unable to speak in the sudden vacuum of silence.

'Mungo,' Lady Ruanthorpe said at last, 'I don't think it's good for Baby to be taking him about among the crowd in this hot sunshine.'

'They want to see him,' Sir Charles said, searching for his grandson through a pair of old, race-meeting field-glasses.

'Don't interfere,' Lady Ruanthorpe snapped. 'There he is over there. Tell Mrs. Crawford to bring him here, where it's cool.'

'It's just because you want him here,' Sir Charles said, without lowering the glasses.

'Well, there's nothing very monstrous in that, is there?'

They were settling down comfortably to one of their customary bickering bouts, when a fashionably dressed, fair woman came forward, elegantly closing her parasol, as she moved into the shade.

IV

'Now, you're Mrs. Arthur Moorhouse, aren't you, my dear? Come and sit beside me,' Lady Ruanthorpe said. 'I don't know how you manage to look so cool,' she added, surveying Bel's stylish garden-party hat, her frills and her ribbons, and deciding that she was much too carefully dressed.

Bel, feeling like an actress who has endured a harassing day, but who, in despite, is somehow managing to wring a good performance from her frayed nerves, took an empty chair and looked about her graciously. She explained that she had been to see Margaret, and opined that Margaret had been most wise not to make an effort to appear today.

Old Sir Charles was giving her broad smiles of approval. He liked pretty women.

'Now, let me see, how many children have *you* got, my dear? And how many are with you today? I *should* know. I must have seen them at lunch. But I'm a silly old woman.'

Bel was preparing to shout a detailed description of her family to her host and hostess, but the band started up again, and there was nothing to do but make a graceful gesture of impotence, sit back, and endure the din. On the whole it was better so. She would, at any rate, have a headache when she got home tonight; but there was no need to add a strained throat to it. At least it was cool here and pleasanter than milling hotly about in the crowd, aristocratic and bucolic, in the park beyond.

Now she could see Mungo coming towards them, pushing his way through, and followed by a stiff old woman in the uniform of a children's nurse; the white streamers of her starched cap floating majestically behind her, as she had in her arms the heir to the Duntrafford estates and all that they stood for. Really, what a fuss these people made about everything! But Bel was impressed. And she was annoyed with herself for being impressed. Charles Mungo Ruanthorpe-Moorhouse was settled between his grandparents amid smiles and signs of admiration, the shattering noise of the band still precluding talk – and Bel was free to look about her once more from her point of distinguished vantage.

Over on the other side of the lawn she could see her husband Arthur deep in talk with an elderly farmer. With him was a sturdy country girl – the old man's daughter, presumably. The girl's looks reminded Bel of someone, for the moment she could not think of whom.

And now here were David and Grace. Their recent marriage had, in consideration of the bride's loss, been a very private ceremony; not even all the family. Although Arthur and herself had been there. David was much as usual, really. Becoming a little more important from being a married man, perhaps; and from the sudden weight of great possessions; showing less tendency, perhaps, to make his old frivolous comment on everything that went on around him; losing his sense of humour a little; becoming stiffer – more of a person; yielding, in other words, to the relentless dictates of the dignified prosperity he had chosen for himself.

Grace, adoring as she appeared to be of the husband on whose arm she was now hanging, seemed tired and a little dispirited, Bel thought. She was glad to see that Lady Ruanthorpe had motioned to Grace to come into the shade and rest. Perhaps there were happy reasons for her fatigue. 'And his name will be Robert Dermott-Moorhouse,' Bel said to herself tartly, reflecting the while how much more sensible it was that her own sons – at the moment, no doubt, inflating themselves shamelessly with lemonade in the marquee – were plain Arthur and plain Tom Moorhouse.

The music stopped abruptly once more, leaving its vacuum of silence, just as Arthur joined them. He had been renewing an old acquaintance. He smiled a deferential greeting to the laird as he came up.

'Who were you talking to, Arthur?' Bel asked.

'That was old Tom Rennie with his other girl. Ye mind Lucy Rennie, that sang in the house at the New Year? Her father.'

Bel started up. 'Oh, I would like to meet them.' She looked at Grace and David and settled back. 'No. It's too hot. Never mind. Funny. You would never think Lucy Rennie would have a man like that for her father. Did he say anything about her?'

'She was back at Greenhead,' Arthur told them. 'She had been ill, or something, and came home for a rest. She just went away back to London yesterday. They wanted her to wait and come here today, but she didna.'

Bel's eyes met David's. Both looked away hastily. Now she was glad that the ear-splitting music had started up again. It made talk impossible. Grace, her straw hat in her lap, was lying back fanning herself. Arthur, Mungo and David stood behind them propped against the silver-grey trunk of the beech-tree. Bel was not surprised to see David presently wander off by himself. It was a good thing Lucy Rennie had not come today. David had never told Bel the end of that story, and she felt she could not press him for it. But she thought she had guessed most of the rest. And perhaps someday, if a confidential moment presented itself, she would ask him. She wondered how much Grace knew. Not much, probably.

At all events David had made the right, honourable and profitable marriage that common sense and the family expected of him, and all was well. That benign Providence that watches over the affairs of the respectable had cracked the whip at the right moment, and he, who had threatened to stray, had been safely headed back into the heart of the prosperous flock. And now, as Bel well knew, David was much too tame, much too conventional, to do anything but stay in the fold.

V

The little path that David followed through the shrubbery was pleasant and cool. The green mosses, the pale, half-curled fronds of fern, the wild garlic and the sprouting grass beneath the rhododendrons, all still damp from yesterday's rain, gave out their woodland perfume.

It was pleasant here among the bushes and

300

under the great trees. The tumult and the noise had become mere rumours. Only the more persistent trumpet notes of the band came to him like far-off echoes. A man could walk at peace here; sense the sharp fragrance of the cool damp air about him; and quiet the smouldering discontents of his heart.

Had she left Greenhead quickly because she had suddenly realised that she must come with her relatives to the Duntrafford celebrations, where she would be certain to meet him? And had she really been ill? And what had made her so? David would have given much to know these things. But he knew he never would. And perhaps it was better not.

His path suddenly brought him to the view-point where Grace and he had stood at New Year time watching the River Ayr boiling down there, far beneath them in the moonlight. But, looking down, David's thoughts were on earlier times, when the water was flowing placidly in the bright sunlight, as it was flowing now; taking its leisured ways among those warm, white-baked stones of the river-bed. There would be minnows to catch down there in the warm shallows, and trout snapping at flies in that dark, dangerous pool that was deep, and beyond the depth of two adventurous farm children.

He remembered how Lucy, on one forbidden expedition, had dared him to swim in that pool; how he had been afraid; and how she had sat down indignantly on the bank, stripped herself naked, plunged in, and swum about triumphantly by herself; how he had been shamed into following her. They must both have been about ten then.

But he had not followed her all the way. He had not been wild, like Lucy. It would not always have been cool and easy to plunge after Lucy Rennie, and swim safely in the dangerous waters she had chosen.

Last evening Grace had hinted that they might both, in the natural course, be the parents of a child. The thought had filled his mind with pleasure all this morning.

What, then, had taken him, that he had stolen away from her now to look down on the sunlit river of his childhood? Seeking with regret for the dreams he would not clothe with reality, even if he could?

There was holiday laughter from the bushes behind him. A young ploughman and his lass came forward hand in hand to look over at the view. As they caught sight of the fine young gentleman who looked so like the more homely Mr. Moorhouse they well knew by sight, they dropped their hands and stood respectfully to one side.

David smiled, bade them a good day, and went to see if his wife was still sitting under the beech-tree.

The publishers hope that this book has given you enjoyable reading. Large Print Books are especially designed to be as easy to see and hold as possible. If you wish a complete list of our books please ask at your local library or write directly to:

Magna Large Print Books
Magna House, Long Preston,
Skipton, North Yorkshire.
BD23 4ND

This Large Print Book, for people
who cannot read normal print,
is published under the auspices of

THE ULVERSCROFT FOUNDATION

... we hope you have enjoyed this book.
Please think for a moment about those
who have worse eyesight than you ...
and are unable to even read or enjoy
Large Print without great difficulty.

You can help them by sending a
donation, large or small, to:

**The Ulverscroft Foundation,
1, The Green, Bradgate Road,
Anstey, Leicestershire, LE7 7FU,
England.**
or request a copy of our brochure for
more details.

The Foundation will use all donations
to assist those people who are visually
impaired and need special attention
with medical research, diagnosis
and treatment.

Thank you very much for your help.